JACKSON

SMOKEJUMPERS

BOOK FIVE

BY EVIE RILEY

Jackson

Smokejumpers

Book Five

Copyright © 2024

Evie Riley

Second Edition

ISBN: 978-1-77357-683-1

Published by Naughty Nights Press LLC

Cover Art By Willsin Rowe

EVIE RILEY

JACKSON

**A convict. A firefighter.
A chance to slay the past and heal a
wounded heart.**

Firefighter Jackson Hall is content with his work in search and rescue with the aerial division in California. He also heads up the Cal Fire Inmate Program.

With his faithful golden retriever by his side, and the animal charities he's dedicated to, he needs nothing else to make him happy.

Preferring life with no-strings-attached entanglements, Jax avoids anything more than hook-ups. That is, until one timid prisoner catches his eye and he finds himself doting on the inmate in ways he never expected.

Ayen Gonzalez was convicted of the attempted manslaughter of his husband, despite the brutal circumstances surrounding his marriage. His past is far less than ideal, and now he just wants to do his time and get out.

As a reward for good behavior, he is given the opportunity to work for an inmate program to be trained to fight forest fires. Ayen is more than happy for the opportunity to escape the prison walls.

Then he meets Jackson and his heart stutters whenever the striking older man comes near. Thing is, Ayen can't quite figure out what he has to offer a man like Jax.

When the program ends, will Jackson be able to set things in motion to right the wrongs of the justice system in Ayen's case? Or will he be stuck waiting three more years for the man he's fallen in love with?

Trigger Warnings: Violence, abuse.

CHAPTER ONE

Ayen

FINALLY BEING ABLE to breathe in the fresh air after being crammed inside of a SAC funded bus had me relaxing almost instantly.

Trees surrounded the training camp in a wide arch, acting as a barrier between us and the rest of the outside world. Not even the cars passing by from the freeway, just a quarter mile from where we'd gotten dropped off, could be heard through the treeline.

After the past two years, this all felt like complete paradise.

"All right, gentlemen! Listen up now," Barlow, one of the four COs that had come with us today, called out. "You're going to be taken into the back of the facility for a safety training course. After that, you're going to be fitted for gear. Do *not* make me have to cuff you and put you back on the bus. Let's be on our best behavior today."

Next to me, another inmate, Tyson, snickered quietly. "Looks like our Newjack is feeling a little twitchy today."

As much as I hated to admit it, I found the comment funny even as I actively fought my smile.

There weren't many COs that came

through our unit that didn't feel like they had something to prove—especially the newbie ones that many of the other inmates, including Tyson, liked to call 'newjacks' for some reason.

A lot of insider slang typically went over my head, and back when I'd first gotten sentenced, I'd questioned practically everything, wanting to learn as much as I could about my new home for the next half decade. I'd learned pretty quickly, though, that asking questions got your ass kicked and soon stopped opening my mouth as much.

Officer Barlow was a lot different, though, in the sense that unlike most newbie COs, he had a tendency to baby us. I understood why, but I had a hunch that since all of us—in this program in particular—were the least violent offenders currently in California State Prison, Sacramento aka SAC, and that his preternatural 'mama bird' instincts tended to kick in.

Today, though, Tyson was right. Barlow seemed unnaturally twitchy and more harsh than usual.

But honestly, I didn't really care. I was just happy to be outside of those fifty-foot barbed wired walls for once.

We were ushered to the back of the property, behind the large main cabin where I assumed our COs and the firefighters for this program would be staying. We had our own cabins, quadruple bunked, right across from that—all of which faced directly toward the mess hall.

I never intended on coming with Tyson, my cellmate, on one of those work release programs. But the minute I'd heard it was for six weeks *and* we'd be out in the fresh air and not stuck inside of some factory, manufacturing license plates or something, I was all on board.

Six firefighters were standing in a half-circle, waiting for us when we finally got to the training site. All of them were dressed in various forms of their turnout gear, with most of them in the typical navy t-shirt and trousers clipped up over their shoulders with suspenders.

I shifted a little in my spot.

Since getting shipped off to prison over two years ago, it'd been a long time since I'd felt any kind of desire. That had been long-since beaten out of me, not just by the harsh prison system but by the person that'd actually gotten me sentenced in the first place.

But damn, did those guys look good in their uniforms. I did have eyes, after all.

"Welcome, gentlemen." A man, tall with broad shoulders, a built chest and an easy smile, nodded to us as a group. "The name's Jackson. I'm going to be your trainer for the next six weeks. We're going to start on the basics for the next few days and see how you all do. Once you've made it past that, then we'll graduate into actual search and rescue drill training. Sound good?"

He didn't wait for the murmur of 'yessir's from our group to begin moving to one of the small training stations. None of us moved, even as he gestured for us all to come closer with a wave of his hand.

We knew better than that. One step out of line and it was back to SAC.

It seemed to have amused our trainer

however, because he soon let out a soft chuckle before turning to Barlow. "You mind?"

Barlow quickly cleared his throat and waved his hand at us. "You heard the man. Go."

Tyson nudged my shoulder, "Come on, roomie," and nodded his head to me as he brushed his way to the front of the pack.

I wasn't so much of a fan of being front and center in a crowd, especially since this jumpsuit already made us all stick out like sore thumbs. But I was also not about to be abandoned by Tyson's overeagerness to get his front row tickets to whatever demonstration we were about to watch.

He was kind of the only friend I had at the moment.

"Like I said..." Jackson squatted down,

his long legs spreading apart to accommodate the thick tree stump in front of him. On top of it were a few tools, a frayed rope, some kind of rock-looking thing, and a dozen smooth pebbles. "We'll be starting with the basics: how to make a fire. To understand how to fight forest fires, you're going to need to know *how* they get started and how easy it is for them to spread."

Up close like this, I could see the salt and pepper strands in Jackson's dark hair, with patches of grey accumulated at both temples, along with the slight lines in his face that expressed his age. He was probably twice my age, which historically speaking had always been my type, and was handsome enough to be distracting.

While talking, he rested both of his forearms on top of his thick thighs, which immediately had my gaze darting away from him. Of all times to be attracted to a man the second I laid eyes on them, it just had to be *now* while I was trying to not fuck this up.

Sometimes life felt like one cruel and twisted joke.

I barely recalled any of the information as Jackson ran through the basics on using a flint (the rock-looking thing) on a dried out fiber (the rope) and then stopping the spread of it with an immovable and inflammable object (the pebbles). It wasn't until I was being tugged away by Tyson over to another station close-by that I realized I'd kind of fucking screwed myself over by letting my mind get distracted.

"Can't believe they're letting us play with fire on the first day. They're nuts,"

Tyson was saying while grabbing at the flint.

I shook my head. "We're low-risk. That's why."

"So says you," he shot back at me.

"I'll just let you take the reins on this one," I said, glancing back over my shoulder to the rest of our sixteen-person brigade.

Most of them were already getting busy with trying to start and stoke their fires, while the other firefighters were walking about and observing. Our COs hung back but had watchful eyes for any of us screwing around.

Belatedly, I caught sight of Jackson turning toward Tyson and I, and slowly rising to his feet, an interested arch to his brow.

I quickly turned back around again,

my cheeks burning. I really hoped he wasn't coming over here to observe us.

That's the last thing I needed—an up close and personal distraction.

"Okay, so he said to strike this on this thing..." Tyson had the flint pressing up against the starter, flicking it a few times. "And then to put it on the rope."

Sparks flew as he struck the starter, but nothing caught. Leaning over the stump, I squinted at what we had on it. "I think you have to press it against the rope while you're striking it."

"Yeah, but that guy didn't do that."

I tried to think back to the display Jackson had out for us and to no one's surprise, my mind was completely blank. All I could remember was how the veins in his arms had flexed when he'd been moving his hands together to strike the flint and catch the rope on fire.

Fuck me... we're so going to fail.

"Maybe use the ends of the rope?" I suggested. Logically, it made sense... right? Less densely packed material for the fire to burn through.

"Oh, you're a fucking genius, pumpkins."

I rolled my eyes at the nickname.

"How we doing over here?" I tensed up at the familiar voice. "Get your flint working yet?"

Jackson hovered behind me, his large body not only imposing but hard to miss.

"Yeah, look at this." Tyson struck the flint once more over the frayed edges of the rope, immediately lighting it on fire. However, it died just as quickly as it'd started, leaving the edges of the rope singed and slightly smoking. "Aw, what the fuck?"

Jackson moved around me and lowered himself to get closer to the stump; one of his knees dug down into the dirt while the other leg was propped up to allow his elbow to rest on it.

"Try again, but this time, make sure you cup your hand around the flame until you can get it to catch properly. The wind out here will blow a flame out quicker than it can catch it. You've got to let yours get enough oxygen first before it can spread up the rope."

As fascinating as the information was, all I could focus on was how deeply *blue* his eyes were. They lingered on me for a moment before quickly darting over to my companion as he struck the flint once more.

Tyson quickly let go of it in order to

cup both of his hands around the small embers forming on the rope. He blew on it softly, letting it smolder just as we'd been instructed, and soon, the rope had a healthy flame eating away at it.

"Very nice," Jackson praised. He leaned forward and quickly huffed the flame out, grabbing the flint and starter. "Why don't we have your partner try it this time."

"Oh..." I held my hands up, shaking them. "No, I'm good. I got the gist of it."

"It helps doing it yourself. Practicing the motions is a lot different than watching."

The way he said that last sentence, for some reason, immediately shot straight down to my groin. I cleared my throat, needing to rid myself of the weirdly dirty thoughts. "Yeah, I'm good."

Ignoring me, he set both of the tools in my hand. "Go on. I'll be right here."

The sub in me wanted to desperately let out a whimper.

I'd clearly been celibate for way too long. Maybe it was biting me in the ass not to have taken Tyson up on his numerous offers of getting off with him after lights out. But the potential for a ticket had never seemed worth it, especially since I'd been determined to have a clean wrap sheet for when I finally got out of SAC.

The felony on my records was already going to make my life hard the second I stepped outside of those doors three years from now. Adding onto it just seemed stupid.

Until now, apparently.

Slowly lowering myself to my knees, I

gripped onto the flint and starter tightly. My hands shook slightly when I held it out toward the rope that was shoved my way by Tyson, whose overly eager smile was more than a little foreboding.

He may have confidence in me but I certainly didn't.

"Remember," Jackson said. "Strike it and then stoke it."

"Right..." I mumbled.

Feeling both sets of eyes on me, I fought the urge to make up another excuse and instead, struck the flint against the starter harder than I meant to. Sparks flew everywhere, causing both men to lean back quickly to avoid getting hit.

"Oh! You got one!" Tyson pointed to the rope.

I dropped the tools in my hand quickly

and cupped both of my hands around the ember, watching as it glowed a deep red.

"Now blow on it," Jackson's voice was nearer to me this time, practically in my ear.

A shiver raced up my spin.

I did as I was told, though, leaning over to blow gently on the ember until it grew brighter. It took a few more tries but soon, it was beginning to smoke, catching the frays that Tyson had burned up with it.

"That's it," came Jackson's voice again, lower this time. "You're doing so good."

I took in one last deep inhale and let it out, encouraging the flame to live. It seemed to do the job a little *too* well, because I soon had a healthy flame that hungrily began to eat up the rest of the frayed edges of the rope, expanding out far enough to burn right against my hand.

With a yelp, I jerked myself back from it.

Jackson acted quickly, taking out some kind of thick towel from the back pocket of his trousers and patting it against the flame, snuffing it out almost instantly. He then full-body turned to me, reaching out with both of his hands.

"Let me see."

He pried my hurt palm away from my body, holding it out into the sunlight where he could see a little better.

The skin was bright pink and already starting to shift into an ugly red where the flame had touched.

It didn't look so bad now, but *fuck* did it hurt.

"We're going to need to patch this up before it gets too deep," he said, his eyes growing serious.

"Um, what—" I didn't even get the chance to finish my sentence before he was tugging me up onto my feet again, still tenderly holding onto my wrist and hand.

With a whistle, he caught the attention of a nearby firefighter, nodding over to Tyson. "Watch him for me? I've got to take this one to medical."

CHAPTER TWO

Jackson

IT WAS MY fault.

I'd gone too far in my teasing and now I had an injured inmate sitting in the medic station with an icepack strapped to his hand while I was rifling through the unit's first aid kits.

It wasn't every day that we got such a pretty looking inmate moved into the program. More often than not, I was dealing with the kinds of guys that you'd never want to cross paths with on a sidewalk in the middle of the day, let alone take home to your mother.

But this one was different.

With his big brown curious eyes, his soft features, and the unsure way he carried himself, he wasn't the typical kind of felon I worked with.

What could such a pretty young thing like him have done in his past to end him up here of all places?

Caught up in a gang, maybe?

The innocent ones always did. And then they ended up doing something stupid and landing themselves behind bars.

A. Gonzalez.

That was the name stitched onto the front of his jumpsuit.

A soft whine, along with a single long scratching drag against it, had me turning toward the door. Shaking my head, I leaned far enough over in the small room to catch the door handle and tug it open. Roxy, my golden, trotted in happily, her tail wagging.

"What, you thought we left you out, huh," I said with a chuckle, and closed the door again.

She panted at me and then turned to our newest companion—Gonzalez.

"You afraid of dogs at all?" I asked him, craning my head back around to look at him tucked into the only chair inside of the medic station. He looked so small in his large oversized jumpsuit, only furthering my curiosity on why the hell he was here.

"Um, not usually?" he said, eying Roxy

warily.

"Don't worry, she's not trained to take down inmates or anything if they decide to run—unless it's after dark." It was meant as a teasing note, but Gonzalez seemed to take it a little more seriously than I meant for it to land, because he stiffened up immediately. "I'm kidding."

Still, he didn't seem to relax at all. He only stared guardedly at my dog.

I really needed to stop teasing this poor kid.

However, the small squawk he let out when Roxy trotted over to him and sat down in order to rest her head in his lap had me smiling. Her doe-eyes glanced up at Gonzalez curiously, watching him as he leaned fully back in his chair to give himself a bit of distance.

"She's a softie. Especially if you feed

her scraps from the mess hall," I said, trying to keep the amusement out of my voice.

What *I* needed to do was to keep my own distance. Getting chummy with an inmate spelled disaster in too many fonts to name.

"Noted," he mumbled.

I didn't have the heart to tell him that Roxy wasn't usually one to hang out around the inmates, choosing to keep a wide berth between herself and them. I wasn't sure when that behavior of hers started, but I didn't really blame her for it.

The guys who came through here weren't the violent type by any means, at least not outwardly, but a criminal always had a certain air about them that was a little off-putting. Despite that, though, Gonzalez didn't seem to possess that trait at all. In fact, it seemed like the complete opposite.

Something that Roxy, along with myself, seemed to have picked up on.

"Here we go," I said, finding the right kit and tugging it off the shelf. "I should've grabbed your hand away from that flame sooner. That's on me."

Truth be told, I'd been distracted—*heavily*—by the enraptured look on Gonzalez's face as he watched his flame turn from small embers into something more tangible. I don't know why, maybe it was because of those doe-eyes or maybe it was that slight smile that he wore. But either way, he'd gotten hurt because of my negligence, and to me, that was just unacceptable.

These guys may have only volunteered to be here in order to win favor with their parole boards, but that didn't mean I was supposed to be lax in my own job at teaching them the proper safety measures when it came to dealing with fire in any capacity.

"It's fine," he mumbled, scooting forward while trying to not disturb my dog.

I grabbed the rolling stool and sat down on it before rolling over to where he was. The small rolling tray next to him was the next thing I grabbed while placing the first aid kit on top of it and popping the top open. It was packed nicely, thanks to Riviera, who'd been in a manic mood all last week while she cleaned the entire station before any of our inmates were dropped off today.

I grabbed the ice pack off his hand and assessed the burn. It wasn't too deep, thankfully caught early, but it definitely was hurting him. The middle was a bright red while the edges were a softer pink. Thankfully, no blisters had formed, though.

"How bad is it?" he asked, looking down at his palm.

"You'll live." I snatched the gauze out of the kit and began to unravel it. "It's a Christmas miracle."

He stared at me curiously in response, which was only encouraging me further to play with him.

I liked a challenge, which in this case, was going to be my downfall. This inmate didn't need me poking at him with my own brand of weird humor.

He was a felon, in prison for something serious, even if it was non-violent. Getting mixed up with that was both stupid and morally egregious. Not just for me, but for him, too.

But damn, was I forming a soft spot.

His hands flexed slightly when I spread the burn cream over the wound, coating it generously. Even if a burn didn't *look* severe on the outside, it didn't mean it wasn't hurting like one and wasn't worse underneath the first few layers of skin.

That was what sucked about burn wounds. Until they looked like your skin was actually melting off, not many people took the pain seriously.

Gonzalez let out a soft sigh once the cream began to soak into his skin.

"How's that feel?" I asked, already knowing the answer.

"Better. I didn't think I had my hand on it that long for it to hurt this bad."

"Well, we're warm blooded. So, even if

you didn't, it doesn't matter. Your body's cooking it from the inside, which is why it hurts."

"Oh." He blinked, finally looking at me again. "Really? That's crazy."

"The body's a weird enigma."

He was quiet as I dressed his burn the rest of the way, making sure to keep the gauze tight enough to not fall off while moving but not so much that it would irritate his healing skin underneath. A fine and delicate line to tread that I was thankfully well versed in.

"There we go. Good as new." I reached over and patted Roxy's head.

Standing up, I collected the kit and stored the unused materials back inside of it before latching it once more.

I probably should've taken more of my time dressing his hand, using it to talk with him as much as I could. Having sixteen other inmates in the program, I wasn't going to get any specific one-on-one time with any of them while they were here.

Not like this, anyway.

However, I had a feeling if I did that, it was going to lead me into not wanting to give him back at all. And that was just something I was going to have to suck up.

He'd be out of here in six weeks and never to be seen again.

"Thanks, nurse," he mumbled.

His words had me whipping around again, my eyes going wide.

Was that a joke back?

His cheeks were tinged a darker hue that looked pretty on his tanned complexion, eyes averted so as to not catch mine.

A grin split across my face. All right, maybe I *would* make up some excuse to keep him here for just a little bit longer—

Just then, the door to the medic station was thrown open and an angry CO was storming inside the tiny room. "What the fuck did you do, Gonzalez?"

Roxy began to bark instantly, clearly uncomfortable with the sudden burst of aggression.

I stepped in front of them both, blocking the CO—Browne, according to his nametag—from advancing any more. "We had a burn situation. I'm cleaning him up now."

Roxy quieted instantly with a small huff.

The CO eyed me. "He was supposed to be escorted by one of us before you took him anywhere. You know that, right?"

JACKSON

That was the problem with COs coming onto my property. They always seemed to want to have a big-dick complex with me and show off in front of the inmates that they were the big bosses in charge and that everyone else around them was to fall in line.

In the real world, outside of the prison system, life just didn't work that way. I, along with the rest of my staff, deserved and would demand respect. It didn't matter that we were dealing with criminals of whatever caliber.

SAC had hired *my* force to run this program and having a bunch of their defunct cops coming in here and stomping their feet when they didn't get there was a sure-fire way of getting them kicked out and replaced with someone else on their squad.

However, at the same time, I didn't want to be having *that* conversation in front of Gonzalez who looked two seconds away from pissing himself in fear.

"Look..." I plastered a smile onto my face. "I get that, but this was an emergency."

"Really," the CO drawled. "Doesn't look like anyone's dying in here."

"That's because I know how to do my job." My smile widened, maybe turning a bit sardonic in the process. "Unless you wanted me to call an ambulance and get EMS involved in *that* mess. I figured this was the best way to avoid the paperwork."

At the dreaded *P-word*, the CO faltered.

"Right... well... he needs to get back with the other inmates."

"Absolutely, I'll have him out as soon as I feed him some pain killers."

Browne narrowed his eyes. "What *kind* of pain killers."

Interesting.

So was Gonzalez here for selling dope on the streets?

That would certainly go along with my gang theory. He must be if I was getting that kind of question. Non-violent was usually like that—drug trafficking or something else that was equally lower on the felony totem.

"Tylenol. Two hundred milligrams," I answered.

The CO slowly nodded, shifting until he could see Gonzalez over my shoulder. "The second he's done with you, you're going back to your cabin. There's uniforms there waiting for you and we'll be doing a head count after a strip search. So don't think about doing anything stupid."

"O-Okay." His small voice answering back had me wanting to crack my knuckles and shove Browne back out into the hallway.

Back down. It's not your place.

Curbing the urge, I folded my arms over my chest instead. "We all good here?"

"Yeah, but I'm standing right out here. He needs an escort," Browne said.

Right, whatever.

"Sure thing." I had the urge to slam the door in his face when he finally stepped back out into the hall, but stopped myself at the last minute.

If anyone were to suspect I was giving any of the inmates special treatment, that would be a one-way ticket back on a bus to SAC. As much as I wanted to spend more time with Gonzalez for god knows what reason, I wasn't willing to risk his small sabbatical of freedom to do so.

I was a selfish bastard, no doubt, but not at the expense of someone else.

He'd clearly worked hard in getting SAC to see him as a non-threat—this program was only available to those kinds of inmates who showed exemplary attitudes while incarcerated.

Hopefully, sometime soon, I'd get to see him again. Though, maybe next time it wouldn't be over an injury.

"Thank you." His voice was quiet as I slipped two Tylenol into his hand, and faced the front of the bottle toward Browne to show him the brand.

"Yeah, no problem." Once the CO nodded to me, I set it down and fished a cold water bottle out of the mini fridge on top of the counter, handing it over. "Just let me know if the pain gets worse and we'll reapply that burn cream again."

He nodded before tossing both pills back and taking a generous swing from the water bottle.

"I appreciate it, thank you." He flashed a little, cautious smile at me.

My heart clenched tight in my chest. Jesus, he really was beautiful. Such a shame he decided to waste his life on doing something stupid and getting himself locked up.

He held his hand out with the water bottle in it, handing it back to me. I shook my head, waving my hand at him to keep it. It was the least I could do for causing him to get burned in the first place, even if it was an accident.

"Let's go, Gonzalez," Browne's gruff voice cut through the room again.

Roxy whimpered softly at him moving, standing up slowly from his chair.

Gonzalez hesitated and then reached down to pat Roxy's head gently.

Her mouth opened, her long tongue lolling out and to the side while she panted at him. His smile widened slightly, clearly amused by my dog and her rather insatiable nature when it came to pats and attention.

"Bye... um..." He glanced over at me briefly.

"Roxy," I said, knowing that's what he was searching for.

"Roxy." He patted her head one last time before stepping around us both and heading out the door to follow his CO.

Roxy turned and whined at me again.

"I know, girl." I squatted, pulling her into a hug while rubbing at her sides.

"We'll see him again soon."
Hopefully.

CHAPTER THREE

Ayen

MY HAND FELT like it burned for the rest of the night.

I tried to not take it as a sign of the days to come—ones where I'd be left coming back to my cabin with more bruises and burns than I'd left with that morning. Sometimes, it felt like a penance; usually during my darker moments while I laid away in bed, staring up at Tyson's bunk as he tossed and turned above me while the distant sounds of the jail settling down for the night echoed around me.

That sort of thing happened a lot when I'd first gotten sentenced. The adjustment had been hard and not just because I wasn't used to having my every move watched or to follow a strict schedule that deviating from got me thrown in the hole for a few days.

I'd never felt such profound loneliness as I did those first couple of weeks. I no longer had my beautiful house, or my annoyingly noisy neighbors, or the garden I'd worked so goddamn hard to tend to while I'd been left for weeks on end playing my dutiful house-husband role.

That small slice of utopia that I'd created for myself had been the only thing that I felt was really *mine.* And yet, I'd flushed it all away in a matter of thirteen minutes.

Some would say it was justified, but the courts had thought differently.

Self-defense only counted if the person who was trying to hurt you was a stranger breaking into your house and not the man you vowed to stick with through thick and thin.

At least I had Tyson to keep me company here, too, or rather, to help with keeping my busy mind occupied and not stuck on a certain handsome fireman and his sweet-as-pie dog.

"How's your hand?" Tyson nodded to my bandages as we sat down at one of the tables inside of the mess hall. He already was digging into his plate of food by the time we both got comfortable.

"It's fine. Still kind of hurts but I'll manage."

He nodded again, shoving another fork-load of eggs into his mouth. Honestly, I couldn't really blame him. We got shit for food back at SAC, so freshly cooked eggs and bacon felt like we'd somehow reached heaven without even realizing it.

I sliced a bite onto my own fork and ate slowly.

While it was true my burn hurt less than it did yesterday, it was still all I could focus on during the night along with watching my back.

The cabin Tyson and I were staying in was also occupied by two other guys, Alvin Richards and Lucas McMurphy. They had been fine enough last night after lights out but I knew better than to trust anyone with my eyes closed and my back facing away from the door.

If there was a bigger lesson in prison than not letting your guard down when you least expected it, I didn't know what was.

Sure, we were all considered non-violent, but desperation made you do crazy things. This was the first time any of us were actually all out on a program like this. Outside of the cabin was a long stretch of forest that was acres deep that, given the right circumstances, anyone could get lost in before our COs were any the wiser.

All of that was purely speculation on my part, of course. But it didn't hurt me to consider all of the possibilities. I was not strong, nor was I adept in any kind of physical combat, so if some kind of fight broke out, I'd be a sitting duck waiting for someone to punch me stupid.

Suddenly, I felt something wet against my ankle.

Jumping away from it, I clutched the side of the table and looked over to see what it was. I spotting a familiar dog wagging her tail as she watched me curiously.

"Yo, what the fuck?" Tyson said.

Relaxing back into my seat, I brushed a hand over Roxy's head a few times, smiling when her tongue began to loll to the side of her mouth.

"Sorry about that," said a voice from behind me. "She doesn't usually run off like that."

My entire body stiffened, but not uncomfortably. No, this was much different as I felt an electric pulse race up my spine.

I felt him before I managed to look up, Jackson's looming presence hovering over me.

"How's your hand?" He nodded down at it.

"Fine," came my automatic response.

I could feel Tyson giving me a weird look, but he kept his comments to himself while shoveling the rest of his food on his plate into his mouth. He was smart to do so or else he'd soon find my shoe kicking him in the shin.

"You sure?" To my surprise, Jackson swung around to my left side—opposite of Roxy—and sat on the stool. "Let me take a look at it."

I didn't fight him when he grabbed my wrist in a firm hold, flipping my hand over until it was facing palm up. My cheeks suddenly felt flushed as my fingers twitched, trying to suppress them from shaking at the contact.

How sad was it that the mere touch of an attractive man was practically making me melt in my seat?

Carefully, Jackson peeled the bandages off of my hand and tossed them onto the table. Roxy's face dug into my lap until her head was comfortably resting nuzzled against my stomach, much like the last time we'd met. I grazed my free hand over her soft fur, letting it distract my mind while Jackson continued to poke and prod at me.

"This doesn't hurt?" he asked, pressing along the outside of the burn where it was still bright pink. "At all?"

I never was any good at lying, especially when it came to pain. And I was sure my wince told him as much. But the alternative was to admit that I'd been up with it all night, and that was a little *too* embarrassing to own up to by now.

He chuckled at me and shifted his body to the side to pull something out of the pouch at his hip. "Good thing I brought this with me this morning."

Jesus, am I that transparent?

He took out the tube of burn cream that he'd used a day earlier and uncapped it with a quick flick of his thumb. The dollop he squirted onto my hand was generous, much more than the one he'd given me yesterday.

Did it really look that bad?

Sure, it hurt like a bitch, but I'd had broken bones that felt worse.

It then occurred to me that he probably wasn't up for dealing with any of the paperwork that would follow me complaining to the work program board if I let it go untreated. I wasn't too aware of what the long-term effects of an untreated burn were, but I doubted he'd want to get questioned by the board about it. Not like they'd ever do anything for *me* but it could cause Jackson and the rest of his crew a headache of paperwork.

Unfortunately, as government property went, we were expendable to only a certain extent. When it came to 'damaging' said property, the kind that could result in some kind of lawsuit, that's when things down the pipeline moved rather quickly in our favor.

It wasn't ever much, but prison healthcare beat the unforgiving nature of being out on the streets without it.

After capping the tube and setting it

down onto the table, Jackson shifted my hand between both of his. His thumbs rolled gentle swirls around my skin, massaging the cream into it thoroughly.

It felt nice as I watched his fingers work, enraptured by them gliding over my skin again and again.

Physical touch was always my weakness, even with my ex. I loved to be touched and not just sexually. To have fingers coarse through my hair, to have a pair of arms wrapped tightly around me, to have a body fit perfectly against the curve of my back.

I missed a lot of it, now that I wasn't allowed to have anything in prison. Tyson had offered a few times to relieve the tension that every man in that facility felt at some point, but I never liked the idea. Sneaking around behind the guards watching in order to get in a quickie felt dirty to me. At least in the way that being used purely for sexual gratification did.

My ex had been my first lover and had spoiled me rotten when we first met. There was a time in my life where I wanted for nothing and those had been the best, most blissful years of my life.

Until he somehow got it into his head that I owed him. That's when the real downfall began.

Jackson worked his fingers up slowly from the tips of mine and down to where the burn in the center of my palm was, coating all of it in a nice thin layer of the cream that began to slowly soak into my skin.

His touch was gentle as he worked, taking the kind of care that I wasn't used to receiving.

"Wow, didn't know this place came with VIP service," Tyson teased.

I shot a glare at him, praying that it would be enough to shut him up. One of these days, Tyson was going to get us both into trouble for spouting off nonsense to the wrong person. If he so much as insinuated anything to the COs about Jackson and I, we'd be pulled from the program faster than either of us could blink.

"How's that feeling? Better?" Jackson fanned out my fingers, completely ignoring Tyson's remarks.

Truth be told, it actually did feel a lot better. There was no more of that uncomfortable pinch that lingered every time I moved it or that dull ache of pain that seemed to flare up right when I finally stopped thinking about it.

I forced myself not to pull my fingers together, wary of spreading the cream too much or getting it caked onto other parts of my skin where it didn't need to be.

"Thank you," I mumbled, avoiding eye contact.

For some reason this entire act, while ultimately innocent on the surface, felt so much more than that. It felt intimate in a way I hadn't been with anyone else since my ex. My touch-starved nature was rearing its ugly head and making me feel things that I really didn't need to be feeling at all.

Let alone toward the head of the damn Cal Fire Inmate Program.

I wasn't sure what Jackson's deal was with seeking me out personally like this—he could've just as well had someone else, a CO most likely, come and get me to bring me to the infirmary to make sure my hand wasn't getting infected.

Instead, he'd gone out of his way to come all the way over to the mess hall and check on me.

At least, that's what it was feeling like. Although, who knew. Maybe he was just there to grab breakfast before training began. My over thinking this entire situation was probably just me blowing out a kind gesture way out of proportion.

The guy was just trying to be nice, probably even pitied me.

I was sure all he saw was some kid who had gotten himself involved in something stupid and wound up behind bars. That's what I would've thought looking at me. I wasn't the typical run-of-the-mill criminal with a hardened past and the faint wrinkles embedded into my face to prove it.

I looked like the kind of person that would have a simple 9-to-5 at a local convenience store and occasionally have trouble reaching the top shelf to stock products. Not have a rap sheet that was fifteen charges long.

Not to mention this guy was most likely married with a gaggle of kids at home. That's what hot guys like him always had waiting for them.

Me lusting after someone like him because I'd been starved of any form of human contact that wasn't in exchange for commissary wasn't his problem. It was mine to deal with and get under control before I did something stupid—like flirt back.

Jackson let go of my hand finally, grabbing the scraps of gauze he'd used on me yesterday.

"You shouldn't need to get that wrapped again. We won't be doing anything strenuous today, just a few demonstrations and then some prep work. But if you feel like you need it to be wrapped for that, stop by with your CO to the medic station and someone will patch you up again."

I nodded, my lips pressed together tightly.

"Just let that cream soak in before touching anything, though," he went on. "It's best to let your body do what it naturally does."

"Thank you," I mumbled again, not knowing what else to say.

Roxy huffed against my stomach when her owner rose from his seat. Her big brown eyes flitted between us both while she continued to stay comfortably stuck on my lap.

Jackson let out an amused chuckle before recalling her back to his side. "You boys have a good breakfast."

My gaze locked onto his back as he left, heading over to the buffet where the spread of food was still laid out and one of the prep workers was standing behind the plate display.

Without realizing it, I let out a slow breath.

"Next time, let me get burned," Tyson said. "I want a hot daddy to rub cream all over *my* hand."

I wrinkled my nose. "You're disgusting."

He laughed loudly.

It had me thinking, though—just who *was* Jackson and why did it feel like every time he came around me, there was this weird tension there?

It had to be in my head.

There was no other explanation to it. This guy was nice and was trying to be a good host while we were on his turf.

What else would he want from me, anyway?

Right?

CHAPTER FOUR

Jackson

TRAINING WENT AS smoothly as it could go considering the fact that none of these inmates had any sort of exposure to firefighter procedures before in the past.

I had to say, out of any of the groups we'd had come through here over the last few years, none of them had ever been as proactive as these guys were.

Sure, there was plenty of bumbling

and knocking things over but aside from that, we had a good group this time around. It was rare to see so much cooperation among a bunch of criminals who were used to doing things in their own way, on their own time—which was most likely part of the reason they were even here in the first place.

But still, it was a nice change of pace for once.

I'd been careful to mind myself when walking around the groups as they'd broken up to practice what they'd learned, keeping a careful distance between me and Gonzalez for the time being.

Whatever had possessed me to walk up to him during breakfast and slather a bunch of burn cream all over him like I was trying to perform some type of fucked up version of a Thai hand massage had me frustrated.

And not just mentally.

Not just for my lack of boundaries that I'd been forcing myself to abide by since he got here, but because seeing his eyes widen at the sight of my fingers carefully moving along the ridges of his hand and working between the tendons had turned me on more than I'd expected it to.

What I wouldn't give to see that same expression while I ran my hands along his body, feeling out which parts of him were oversensitive and watching him squirm when I finally found them.

It was fucked up—all of it. Yet my mind had completely attached itself to the idea and no matter what I did, it continued to play over and over again. A non-stop loop that was driving me fucking mad. I kept rolling the fantasy over and over in my head as I made my rounds and steered clear of him and his friend.

What I actually needed to do was head to the bar after this and go get laid.

Clearly, I was pent up for whatever reason and needed to clear my head. Once I was done, I could come back to the station clear-headed and focused and not continue to obsess over a pretty little inmate that I was growing suspicious of being a sub.

Because what else would he be with how obediently he'd let me touch him and seemed to lean into the heat of my body so close to mine?

Ugh.

Fuck...

When the sun finally set, we called it enough for the night.

Inmates filed into the mess hall to grab dinner and settle down for the rest of the evening while I headed to the staff cabins to grab my things. During these programs, I tended to opt for staying on property. More as an ease of convenience than anything else. My house was more in the city and battling traffic everyday just to arrive at the ass crack of dawn was bad for my blood pressure.

Tonight, though, I'd stay in the city and deal with fighting my way back to the sticks in the morning. It was worth it in the end if it got me to stop focusing so heavily on Gonzalez and take my desires elsewhere.

A casual hookup hadn't ever failed me from working out my frustrations in the past.

"Going somewhere, Hall?"

I looked over to my colleague, Ryan, as we entered the staff section of the training grounds. "Yeah, into the city."

He raised a brow at me. "You're going back home for the night? That's rare."

"No, just the bar. You want to hitch a ride?"

He laughed and slapped me on the back on our way in through the doors of the main pavilion. "Not a chance. Last time I went with you, I could barely function the next day. You drink like a fucking ox and my liver can't handle that right now."

"Least I got you laid," I quipped back and headed into the locker room. Mine was toward the back of the row with a beat up looking door and a lock that liked to jam on me sometimes. I found mine and quickly rotated the dial for my combo.

"Yeah, as well as a concussion from falling face first on the pavement the next morning from my hangover."

"Hey, that was *after* your hookup," I pointed out. "So, I'm still taking credit for a job well done."

My locker creaked as I opened it. Stripping out of my gear and hanging it up, my shoulders began to relax instantly. Rolling them back a few times felt nice, along with my neck cracking on each side as I rotated it.

Next to me, Ryan pulled open his own locker. The bright fluorescent lights above us bounced off his bald head, still slightly slick from sweat from being under his helmet all day in the hot California sun.

Even though up here in the more forested parts of Sacramento was a lot cooler than in the city, we still got those massive heat waves that were brutal under all of our gear. These past few days we could get away with the bare minimum coverage but starting next week, some of us were going to need to gear up completely when the real training began.

"Have fun on your escapade," Ryan shot back. "Just make sure you're still functionally drunk when you come back tomorrow. Wouldn't want you to get burned like that inmate."

His chuckle had my hand clenching around the side of my locker door tight enough to hurt.

A harmless joke, that's all it was. There was no need for the sudden anger that flared through my chest. I probably still had some residual guilt left over from the incident brewing in me that was causing me to have such a knee-jerk reaction.

Gonzalez was fine.

Honestly, his hand looked almost healed aside from the still pinkened skin when I last saw it.

During training today, he hadn't made a peep at all.

Not that I was really paying attention to him to notice.

Still, he was an adult. If he really needed medical attention, he knew how to get it.

I ignored the small voice in the back of my head that whispered doubt about that—given his shy and passive nature. I had to trust that if there was something going on with him, either someone else would notice or he'd actually pull on his big boy pants and deal with it.

Chewing at the inside of my cheek, I slammed my locker shut a little harder than necessary.

"You good there, Hall?" Ryan raised a brow at me again.

"Yeah. I'll see you tomorrow," I said as I waved and headed back to my cabin to change into something more fresh and say goodbye to Roxy for the night.

I hadn't felt this kind of protective instinct over a man like Gonzalez in a long ass time and it was really beginning to throw me for a loop.

He reminded me so much of my cute little submissives that I loved to take back home with me from the clubs I frequented all throughout my twenties. Back then, I had a lot of misplaced emotions over what had been going on at home.

Being a young, gay college kid who'd

been essentially disowned by his only parent had rocked my world more than I really ever realized until later in life.

I'd wanted to save the subs I took home. Do the one thing for them that I'd wished someone had done for me.

Learning the hard truth that not everyone wanted that had been a long and grueling lesson. In the end, I'd turned my passion toward firefighting, teaching new recruits, and rehabbing criminals through work placement programs.

It was better this way. It kept me busy and I got to see people strive to meet their goals and push them until they were across the finish line instead of trying to placate myself in another relationship with a doomed timeline.

Roxy growled happily at me as I entered my cabin, a toy stuffed in her mouth while her feet tapped against the hardwood floor. I swept my hand over her head a few times before shedding my sweaty clothes for something fresher.

Tonight was all about getting my head back on straight. No more of this obsessing over an inmate business.

CHAPTER FIVE

Jackson

THE BAR WASN'T as nearly packed as I
wanted it to be, but I supposed that's
what I got for coming in on a Wednesday
night.

Thankfully, by the time I was served
my second beer, I spotted a cute blond
over in the corner of the bar hanging out
by the pool table. He had on a pair of
short-shorts that were frayed at the ends

and a cropped top that didn't quite show off his full mid-drift but did tease a little bit of skin. His hair was messy, tossed on top of his head, giving him that 'barely put together' look that was so in right now.

Tossing back the rest of my drink, I left the glass on the bar and slid off of my stool to head over to him.

He was on his phone, scrolling for something, his bottom lip pinched between his teeth.

"You up for a round?" I asked, grabbing one of the cue sticks off of the rack.

He looked up, his eyes widening briefly before he grinned. "Oh. Yeah, sure. But you're going to have to teach me."

"My pleasure." I flashed him a smile.

After handing him one of the sticks, I

moved closer to the table and snatched the blue chalk cube up to rub on the tip to freshen it up a bit. With a wink, I tossed it lightly at him and said, "I'll take stripes."

Lining up my cue, I pinned it back twice before striking the rack, sinking two of the stripes balls into the left-most pocket.

He let out a gasp and clapped. "Wow! Impressive. I didn't know I was in the presence of a seasoned expert."

The way he said it had me snorting softly to myself.

Sometimes the younger ones liked to put me in a box. I think it was my refusal at dyeing my hair and letting my grays grow out instead of trying to pretend like I wasn't forty-five. I wasn't so much attached to ages as long as whomever I was with was at least in their mid-twenties.

Anything below that and I ran the risk of a clinger.

"Mind showing me?" he said, coming closer to me with a sway of his hips.

He was hot, I'd give him that.

He pressed himself against the lip of the table and bent over, sticking his ass out, and very poorly secured his cue on top of one of his hands.

I chuckled, getting up in his space in order to correct his posture using my hands on his hips as a guide.

"Try that instead. And hit the solid colored ones, or else I'll win," I said.

He grinned at me over his shoulder. "And what happens if you do?"

"How about I take you home?" I moved his hips again, fixing the way his body was tilted before I let him go again.

"I like the sound of that," he said before whacking his cue against one of the balls closest to him.

While I meant what I said, there just wasn't any heat behind my promise. Sure, the kid was hot and would most likely be a fun time, but for some reason I wasn't feeling it.

Maybe I needed another drink in me. Or maybe I'd been spending way too much time in the sun.

"*Oh*, did you see that? I hit one," he said, standing back up.

As he turned, he pressed his entire body against mine. His cute little cock was already hard and rubbing against mine. "How about we skip to the part where you win and take me home."

Man, how easy would it be to take him

up on his offer?

I cupped his face, squeezing slightly as I looked down at his round features.

The only problem was that this kid's eyes were a soft blue and not the deep rich brown that I was hoping they'd be. There was a dusting of pinkish makeup around his eyes, bringing out the blue even more. His skin was pale, not the tan that I'd been fantasizing about running my tongue over to taste how salty it'd be after along day of working under the scorching sun.

Fuck.

What a damn bust.

"Sorry," I said, letting him go. "I just remembered I've got a thing in the morning."

He pouted. "Seriously?"

"Rain check?" I asked, even though

both of us knew this would be the last time we'd see each other.

"Yeah," he waved his hand, rolling his eyes and pulling out his phone again. "Sure. Whatever."

I pecked him on the forehead as an apology. "Hope you find someone to take you up on that offer."

He smiled a little, waving me off again. "Go away before I make you take me home."

I had to laugh at that.

Setting my cue stick back on the rack, I headed out and climbed into my truck.

Well, so much for trying to fuck my energy out with a stranger. I didn't typically like to resort to using my hand but apparently, that's where this was headed tonight. At least with masterbating, I wouldn't have to pretend to replace the features of one man for another.

Getting back on property was easy with the late-night traffic. Soon enough, the familiar wooden sign stating 'CAL FIRE INMATE WORK PROGRAM' greeted me.

I parked my truck and killed the ignition just as something flashing caught my eye.

Two COs were running together with their flashlights bobbing on the ground, followed closely by two of my guys who were sprinting after them.

My heart hammered in my chest as I kicked my door open.

Fuck, were they heading for the inmate cabins?

I slammed my door shut and ran after them, hoping like hell I was wrong.

CHAPTER SIX

Ayen

I WINCED AS cards were tossed onto the floor.

"You motherfucker!" McMurphy shouted, standing up to hover over the other man. "I saw you sneak in another card! You think this is fucking funny, don't you?"

"Fuck off," Richards snapped back, shoving McMurphy away as he stood. "I didn't sneak fucking shit! You're just shit at the game.”

I shuffled back from where they were, slowly inching myself toward the corner of the room that was as far away from them as possible.

The night had started off simple enough—a card game to pass the time after lights out. Richards had apparently snuck in a deck from SAC and stashed it under his bunk mattress until the COs had retired for the night.

We—Tyson and I—had figured, what was the harm in a few rounds of cards?

It wasn't like there was anything to bet that would get anyone heated.

Apparently, that had been dead wrong because halfway through the second game, McMurphy had tossed a few cigarette butts down in the center of our card game while saying he'd swiped them up from the ground after one of the COs, Matthers, had been busy chain smoking behind the mess hall.

To me, it seemed rather nasty to suck on the remnants of a used butt just in the hope that there'd be some nicotine left, but apparently I was in the minority with that opinion.

"Calm down, both of you," Tyson hissed, quickly kicking the butts under one of the bunks before standing, too. "You're going to get us kicked out."

"Fuck you, Asper! You want to fucking fight about it?" McMurphy suddenly turned his rage away from Richards and onto Tyson.

"What the fuck is your problem, man?"

"I don't have a fucking problem." He shoved my cellmate back hard, causing him to stumble.

"Oh, no you fucking didn't," was all Tyson said before he swung.

I scrambled up from the floor right as both Tyson and McMurphy slammed down onto it. My heart pounded hard in my chest as I froze, not knowing what I could do to even help Tyson. I wasn't good at fighting, or hurting anyone for that matter.

They both rolled around on the floor, trading blows with each other hard enough for thuds to be heard as fists smacked against skin and bone. I winced at every single one of them, trying desperately to look for a way to break them up without jumping headfirst into the fray.

Tyson's fist shot up to grab at the sheets on the lower bunk next to me, trying to pull himself up off the floor. Both the top blanket and sheet ripped away from where it had been tucked against the wall and shifted across the bed messily as he tried to stand up.

The give in it wasn't enough, though, and soon sent Tyson flying back down onto McMurphy's chest.

Richards lifted his foot to slam it down onto my cellmate, and instantly, I had my hand wrapped around my pillow and tossed it at him.

It barely had any effect aside from getting him to look up at me when it hit him and turn that scowl into a downright snarl.

"You have something you wanna say, Gonzalez?" he spat out.

My arms flew over my head instinctively, years of this same situation suddenly flashing through my mind, mirrored by what was going on. Soon, I'd be hit in the back or on the arm hard enough to break the protective hold I had over my face. The force of it would stun me enough to pry my arms apart and next a fist would come flying at my face, upper cutting me hard enough to rattle my teeth.

That's how it always went. I'd be back in the damn house with no one but my oblivious neighbors to hear my screaming.

My breaths hitched in and out of my chest hard as I waited for the familiar blows. My entire body shook as I hunched in on myself, praying that it would be over soon.

A crash coming from the front of the cabin had me sinking to my knees instantly, practically curling up in a ball on the floor as panic began to take over.

"What the fuck is going on in here!" someone shouted. "Get the fuck up off each other!"

There was some more arguing and what sounded like a couple of our COs breaking up the fight. I didn't dare to peek, though, afraid that I'd be met with a fist to my eye and a concussion to follow.

"Jesus," someone said over me, a familiar voice, laced with worry.

Worry?

"Gonzalez?"

My entire body was most definitely shaking visibly.

Oh god, was I going to get shipped back to SAC?

Only two days into the goddamn program?

I was never going to get another work program like this if I got sent back. No board was going to look at my record and cut me some slack if they thought I was involved in some fight.

Hands came around to grab at my wrists in a gentle hold, pulling at them. "Hey, come here."

I was frozen solid, stuck in the protective position while I rode through my panic attack. That was the shitty thing about having PTSD, it came at the worst fucking times.

The hands let go of me and instead, I felt a pair of arms wrapping around my body and quickly plucking me up from the floor. Instinctively, my fingers latched onto the hard muscles of the shoulder I was thrown up onto, holding me tight to the person that was carrying me.

"Hey, it's okay," he said, patting my back. "You're all right."

A soft noise escaped my lips.

I was carried through the cabin and out into the cool night air. Breathing in deeply, I caught a familiar spicy scent that had me relaxing almost instantly. Back inside the cabin, I could hear the COs yelling, something about illegal gambling.

"Gonzalez." I was carefully swung back down onto my feet and Jackson's face suddenly appeared in front of me. "What happened?"

"I... um..." I tucked my arms tight around my body, holding myself while I shook.

He shrugged off his jacket and draped it over my shoulders. The inside of it was warm and had his scent practically melted into the seams. I nuzzled my face against the collar, letting the spicy smell of him soak into my bones and bring me back down.

"Were you guys gambling or something?" he asked.

I shook my head.

He didn't seem like he was judging me, at least from the tone of his question.

Well, I guessed that was kind of a lie, though. Just because I wasn't directly involved in the gambling didn't mean it wasn't going on and that I wasn't exactly participating in it. I wasn't after the prize but I was still slapping down my cards in order to up the pot's stakes. I personally wasn't playing to bet on a couple of used up cigarettes, but that didn't mean the other three weren't.

By association, I was guilty, too.

The one thing about prison life was that we were an all-for-one society, even if none of us believed in it. Privileges were either given or revoked due to other inmates behavior and when one of us fucked up, the rest suffered.

That was why the violence rates could get pretty bad. If there was one bad apple that was making life unbearable for everyone else, he needed to be taken care of.

By all intents and purposes, whatever happened to McMurphy, Richards, and Tyson in there was going to become my fate, too.

"Gonzalez?" Jackson asked again.

"Ayen," I said quietly, mumbling it into the fabric of his jacket.

"What?"

"*Ayen.* My name."

His eyes widened briefly.

After tonight, I would never see this

man again. Might as well leave him with a little piece of me. Not that he'd really care. All I was to him was a number and a vaguely familiar face.

Before he could say anything back, one of the COs, Stinner, came stomping out the front door of the cabin. "Gonzalez!"

I winced and quickly hid behind Jackson.

To my surprise, the man shifted just enough to block me entirely from the COs view.

"He wasn't doing anything," Jackson said. "You know that, right?"

"He was fucking gambling! That's against the rules."

"He was cowering in the corner trying not to get hit. My bet is that he was probably asleep when all of that went down."

My gaze shot up to stare at the back of Jackson's head.

Why was he defending me?

To a CO no less?

What could he possibly be getting out of it?

"Go look at how messy the bed he was next to was," Jackson went on. "The sheets were pulled back and everything."

Stinner let out a loud scoff but didn't argue. "Whatever. We need to separate all of these guys for the night. The bus won't be able to get out to us until morning."

"I've got a spare staff cabin. One of them can bunk with me, there's an extra bed. I'll take Gonzalez since he had nothing to do with this."

My jaw dropped open.

Wait, was he serious?

"We're going to have to discuss that

with the other COs," Stinner was saying, but Jackson was already reaching back to grab my arm.

"That's fine. I need to go open up the medic station so we can get those other two checked out. Unless you want to call an ambulance?"

I bit the inside of my cheek to keep from grinning.

The dreaded 'A'-word. Every CO's worst nightmare.

Not only would the prison be held responsible for the inmates' care while there, they'd also have to ship out a few COs in order to guard the doors to make sure no one got the bright idea of slipping out of their room and getting out onto the streets.

And literally *no one* wanted guard duty in a hospital. Not only was it boring as all hell to wait outside of a patient's room twiddling your thumbs, but I doubted any of them would be getting overtime.

Not with the way our Warden worked.

"Yeah. Sure. We'll meet you over at the station with them," Stinner said. "He needs to be handcuffed, though."

Jackson sighed, dropping my hand. "All right."

I held out my still shaking hands to Stinner, who slapped a pair of cuffs on them, wrenching them tight enough to hurt when I moved my arms around. He was one of the COs that was known to be in a pissy mood if things like inmate fighting cut into his 'me time' away from all of us.

Jackson finally took me by the wrist again and led me away from the cabins.

The lights coming off of the buildings

we passed by gave us just enough illumination to see where we were going but not enough to look like we'd stepped out onto the center of the sun.

As we grew farther and farther away from the cabins, my heart began to slow and I could breathe again.

Jesus, I hadn't been that up close and personal to a fight since I first came to SAC. My first week there had been quite the initiation into prison life, with a guy in my unit being stabbed and another one being dragged out and beaten up in the yard during our rec period while I'd been standing close by.

After everything that had happened leading up to me being arrested and going to jail, I'd never had a good track record with being met face-to-face with aggression or imminent threat.

The one time I'd defended myself had landed me in prison. So...

"You okay?" Jackson turned back to look at me right as we reached the medic station.

I swallowed thickly. "Yeah. I, uh... I hope you don't think I was involved in any of that."

Why did I say it like that?

And why would Jackson even care?

Did I *want* him to care?

It wasn't like his opinion of me should matter. If it did... well, it'd just complicate things.

Right?

"Oh..." He lifted a hand and very gently dragged his fingers through my hair, brushing it back away from my face. "No, not at all. You're far too sweet to be involved in any of that."

My entire body flushed with heat as the air in my lungs caught in my throat. I was so glad it was dark out there because I was sure my face was bright red with how hard I was blushing.

What the hell did that even mean?

His thumb traced along my forehead before dropping back down to his side. "Let's get you cleaned up."

CHAPTER SEVEN

Jackson

AYEN.

What a pretty name. It was fitting for someone who looked and acted like him.

I ran my gaze over him, taking in his curious expression as he wandered around my cabin. One of his hands gripped at his wrist, rubbing over the red ring that had been left from the too-tight cuffs.

I'd somehow managed to convince his CO to take them off before bringing him to my cabin after I'd gotten the medic station opened up—another thing that I was surprised they went along with. I had a good track record with them, though, and technically, this was *my* program. So my rules typically superseded whatever they had bickered about amongst themselves.

SAC got a good tax write off by working with my program—inmate rehabilitation was all the rage and made for good bragging rights when it came time for the Warden to be schmoozing it up with the governor about how well their programs were running and raking in the grant money when the fiscal new year rolled around.

Mine had one of the better success rates, so pissing me off and cutting SAC loose would be detrimental.

Which was probably why I got my way tonight.

"You can take the bed." I nodded to the door that was closed just down the hallway. "I'm fine with the couch."

Ayen whipped around with wide eyes. "I can't *take your bed*. I thought you had a spare?"

"I lied." I grinned. "I promise, I don't have cooties."

His cheeks visibly flushed a cute light pink in the soft lighting of my cabin.

It was a nice place, with a full sized bedroom, kitchen, living room, and small dining room. There was a reason I didn't mind staying here during the entire program. Compared to pretty much everyone else on the property, I was living it large.

"I—that's…" he stuttered. "That's not what I meant."

I walked over to him slowly, my dick stirring as I watched him track my movements. I hated seeing him so afraid back in his cabin while that fight was happening. Thankfully, by the time we'd come gotten here, he'd perked up a bit. I never wanted to see him like that again; not on my watch at least.

How bad had prison been for him to have that kind of reaction?

I didn't want to think about it—if I did, it was only going to make me mad.

Instead, I grabbed his wrist and pulled it from where he'd been stroking it with his hand. I ran my thumb lightly over the irritated skin, the ridges of where the cuff had been digging into him instantly annoying me.

JACKSON

The COs that came in here with their aggression barely in check were always the ones that pissed me off the most. Not because they were particularly more of an asshole than the rest, but because they took all those pent-up feelings out on the inmates who were only trying to learn, and hopefully, make something of themselves when they finally got out.

"I think I'm going to have to wrap you up in bubble wrap from now on," I murmured.

He huffed out a laugh. "I don't think that's the take-away from all of this."

"Let me at least put some ointment on this. Should heal you right up." I couldn't help the need to care for him. It was a burning desire that was blooming in my chest and only seemed to get worse the longer I stayed in his presence.

Touching him in any capacity was beginning to become addicting—so much so that I was trying to make up any little excuse to justify myself.

"No, it's okay." He stayed rooted to his spot, even as I tugged at him to follow me to the bathroom. "You've done enough as it is."

"Are you sure?" I didn't want him to say yes. I wanted him to let me take care of him.

But, of course, he merely shook his head and slipped his wrist out of my grip.

I wanted to argue but he'd already been involved in enough tonight. My pressing him to do what I wanted him to do was only going to create a weird dynamic between us that I didn't want to happen. I already had him out of his element and in *my* space. There was no sense in pushing his boundaries while I was trying to make him feel more comfortable.

"You want water or anything?" I stepped away from him and headed into the kitchen. I flexed my fingers together at my sides while I mourned the loss of having them wrapped around him in some capacity.

Right now, I was really starting to regret not taking that cute blond home and fucking his brains out because this was getting to be ridiculous.

How was it that an inmate that I hardly knew could render me into such a goddamn needy mess?

I heard him follow me by the sound of the old and worn floorboards creaking slightly under his feet. "I'm okay."

Even with his refusal, he still was

seeking out my company. That had me smiling a little bit to myself.

Jesus, I needed to get it together.

Turning back around, I fixed him with a look over my fridge door as I pulled it open. "Not even if it's ice cold?"

He let out another soft laugh—a delightful sound. "Is this you not taking *no* for an answer?"

Yes.

"Well, only when it comes to hydration." I slipped a bottle out from the top shelf and handed it to him. "I never play about that."

He uncapped it and took a generous swig. My coat looked massive still hanging off his shoulders and dwarfing his already petite frame. But somehow, it looked good on him.

Really good.

Right, even.

It had me thinking about putting him to bed in one of my t-shirts next.

My stomach clenched at the thought, possessiveness rearing its ugly head once more.

I wanted to keep him here permanently but there was no way the COs were going to allow that. Chances were that as soon as the sun was up, a bus would be rolling by to pick all four of them up and ship them back off to SAC for poor conduct.

It hurt my heart to think that Ayen would be caught up in all of that when it was obvious to anyone with two fucking eyes that the poor kid was way too scared to even be involved in any of that drama. Maybe he had been fucking with the cards initially, but I highly doubted he instigated that fight or was ever involved in it in any capacity.

I couldn't see him as the type.

Especially with how I'd found him curled up in himself while he shook through his panic attack.

Fuck, seeing him like that had really upset me. More than I cared to admit. He wasn't supposed to be scared here, none of the inmates were. So walking into *that* and seeing him shielding himself like he was ready for someone to start wailing on him had me tearing through that damn cabin in order to get to him.

Getting him out of there had been my only priority. Getting him to safety—to *me*—was the single thought that had been rattling through my brain.

Ayen capped the half finished bottle again and stared at it for a long moment while I leaned against the door of my fridge, watching him. The cool air from it felt nice against my skin even though it wasn't that humid out tonight.

"Why... are you doing all of this?" He glanced up at me. "I... You defended me to Stinner..."

I shrugged. "He was being an ass."

Which was true, in a sense. That CO coming out of the cabin hot and ready to pick a fight had my protective instincts flaring instantly. There was no way I was going to let Ayen go with him when he was already scared. Turning him over to a CO like that would keep me up all fucking night worrying about him.

Ayen frowned at me. "But he's the CO... it doesn't really matter what his attitude is like. Aren't you supposed to... Uh—" He cut himself off, his lips pressing together tightly.

"'Listen to him?" I guessed. "Not at all. He's in my neck of the woods."

"You own this place?" His eyes widened in curiosity.

Damn was he cute.

I fisted my hands together, pretending they were holding onto him.

"Kind of. I run the program and have been for a decade." I lifted away from the fridge door and let it swing shut.

His eyes widened more. "Wow, that's amazing."

"Thanks. It's been quite the wild ride."

"I bet tonight has added to that list..."

I shrugged. "They weren't the first to fight on the property and they won't be the last. Sometimes it happens when you give someone a little too much freedom too soon."

He nodded slowly, looking back down

at his water bottle with a concentrated look on his face. I wondered what my words meant to him.

Did he relate?

Was he the type of person to not know what to do with the freedom given to him?

Clearly his trouble with the law had been something like that—as all criminals were.

Freedom was what you made of it. It could give you everything and it could take away everything. It all depended on your choice with what to do with it.

To be honest, since meeting him, I'd been insanely curious as to what his charges were. As a non-violent offender, they weren't anything heinous like sex crimes or murder. But I couldn't see Ayen being a drug runner or something like that—he was too sweet, too soft around the edges that people in the drug business didn't have.

Whatever it was, I wanted to know. Not even just for my own curiosity's sake but to better understand him, too.

What had caused him to lose his freedom in the first place and what was he willing to do to get it back?

This program was the first step.

What would be his next?

Ayen's voice was quiet as he said, "Thank you."

I smiled. "You're welcome."

"You never answered my question, though." His eyes met mine again. "Why are you doing all of this?"

"Why can't I?" I challenged.

His brows pulled together. "What do you get out of it? I can't really give you anything."

A dark part of me whispered that there were *plenty* of things he could give me but I quickly clamped that down.

I wasn't interested in coercing him into bending over and letting me touch every inch of him. He was my unattainable grail.

"Look, I may not know you or anything, Ayen, but I can tell the type of person you are. My gut says you would never intentionally hurt someone."

For some reason, a sad look passed over his face and his gaze dropped down to the floor where he stared at his feet. The silence between us was both startling and strange, and had me wanting to ask him what happened before I bit my tongue and stopped myself from doing so.

Whatever it was, it was probably none of my business. He didn't owe me anything, even if I had gone out of my way tonight to protect him. If he wanted to tell me in his own time, then he was free to do so. I'd never push anything.

I'd done that out of my own selfish need to keep him safe and nothing more.

"Why don't you go rest up for the night," I said to break up the tension. "Seems like tonight's already been long enough."

"But, the bed..."

I cut him off by grabbing him by the shoulders and spinning him around. He didn't fight me at all when I led him through my cabin and down the hallway to my bedroom.

"I'll survive for one night," I said, and opened the door for him. "Get some sleep."

He looked like he wanted to argue with

me but soon thought better of it at the last moment. A small sigh escaped him when he finally relented.

"All right... Thank you, I appreciate it."

"Of course." I smiled and stepped back.

I itched to touch him again—to run my fingers through his hair or cup his face and press a goodnight kiss to his forehead before he headed off to bed. Anything that would bring him closer to me so that I could feel his body heat soaking through my thin t-shirt.

I forced myself to hold my smile. "I'm going to have to keep the door open, though. Just in case one of your COs decides to pop in and do a check."

"Oh. Yeah, of course."

"All right..." I backed away slowly down the hall. "Holler if you need anything."

"I will. Thank you."

I flopped down on my couch and let my elbows rest on my knees as I watched the shadows of his figure dance in the light spilling out into the hallway from my overhead light. I laced my fingers together in a tight hold, squeezing them together while I kept my inappropriate thoughts to myself.

What I wouldn't give to join Ayen in that bed right about now. Cuddle up behind him and pull him against my chest and see how well his body fit against mine.

Would we be tangled up awkwardly or would he scoot back enough to let me perfectly curl around him?

Ah, fuck.

I need to stop this train of thought before it got out of hand. Or rather, before

I needed to put my dick *in* my hand. Because masturbating while in full sight of Ayen if he glanced out the bedroom door was not going to happen.

I sighed. For now, I'd just have to settle myself with the fact that he'd be tucked between my sheets and hopefully, getting his scent all over them—mixing with mine.

Tomorrow, I'd let my fantasies run wild.

Tonight, I'd get some shuteye and deal with what judgment came in the morning.

CHAPTER EIGHT

Ayen

I SLEPT WELL that night, surrounded by a comfortable bed and pillows that felt like heaven against my face.

It'd been two long years since I'd slept on a proper mattress with actual back support and not the flimsy material of my foam mattress back in my cell with a steel bed frame underneath it. Two long ass years since I'd actually felt well rested by the time I finally blinked my eyes open in the morning.

I stretched my arms over my head and sank further into the covers surrounding me. Jackson's scent was all over them, enveloping me in him just like his jacket had. I savored it all, memorizing it for when I was back in my cellblock at SAC later on today when the bus finally came to pick us all up and bring us back.

As sad as it was to be leaving this place after only a few days, I couldn't say I regretted any of it.

Especially meeting Jackson.

I was never going to see the man again after this, and while that kind of choked me up inside, at least I was able to see him one last time before leaving. It seemed so silly to be lusting after a man I barely knew in the grand scheme of things—but even if it was just the idea of him that I had been enamored with, that was something that I would cherish for the rest of my time while I was locked up.

The entire time he'd been nothing but kind to me, going out of his way to help me when he was never asked to. He was a good man, one that anyone would be lucky enough to know, let alone be with.

Sitting up, I peeled back the covers and climbed to my feet. My entire body cracked, easing the tension in my bones almost immediately.

Damn, I was going to miss this bed.

There was a delicious smell wafting from down the hallway that I found myself following. I spotted Jackson in the kitchen cooking something over the stovetop. His shirt was off and he was in just a pair of sweats that did everything to highlight the kind of assets he had.

Jesus, as if my lusting for him wasn't bad already.

Most likely feeling me staring, he glanced over his shoulder at me and flashed me a smile. "Morning."

I blinked a few times, trying to clear the image of his body now ingrained into my brain. Roxy lifted herself up from where she'd been laying down on the floor over by the dining table and trotted over to me, her tongue hanging out of her mouth as she panted happily.

I bent down to pet her before turning back to Jackson. "What time is it?"

He glanced over at the clock before answering. "Just after eight."

My eyes widened. "I need to get over to the bus."

"Woah, woah, woah." He grabbed my

arm just as I was starting to head for the door. "It already left."

"*What?*"

Oh fuck, fuck, fuck.

I was in such deep shit.

"Yeah, about two hours ago."

If there wasn't solid ground under my feet, I had no doubt I would've melted into the damn Earth.

Fuck, I was in *so* much trouble.

Why the hell didn't the COs come looking for me when the bus had come?

Could they not find me?

It wasn't like they had a giant headcount to keep track of. There were only four of us! As soon as SAC found out I was still here, I was going to be thrown in the hole the second I got back.

Anxiety spiked inside of my chest at the thought.

I'd only been there once and it had been the worst three days of my life. I never knew that I was the kind of person who needed human interaction in order to survive but I sure learned that weekend.

"Ayen..." Jackson's voice jerked me out of my thoughts. "You're all right. The bus already left."

"That's the *problem*." I could hear the shaking in my voice. "I was supposed to be on it."

He shook his head. "No you weren't, honey. You're staying here at the program."

Wait, what?

I stared at him, trying to find the hidden joke that he was trying to tell.

Was this some kind of prank?

A test?

To see if I'd go along with it and not

correct him, therefore making it seem like I was taking his word over my COs?

They'd be the type to do that fucked up shit.

Especially Stinner.

Oh fuck.

Roxy whined at me, her nails tippy-tapping against the hardwood floor as she shifted foot-to-foot.

Jackson set down the wooden spoon he'd been using to move around whatever was in the pan and then turned the burner off. When he faced me, he cupped his hand around my face, tilting it up to look at him.

"You didn't get left behind by accident, if that's what you're thinking."

I blinked at him again.

Wait, what?

He smiled a little. "I talked with the

Warden this morning when he called and explained what I saw last night. He agreed that it wouldn't be in the program's best interest to punish you when you had nothing to do with the fight."

My mouth fell open.

What?

He went out of his way to talk to the *Warden?*

His thumb trailed along my cheek gently, sending a shiver up my spine. His touch was so gentle that it made me want to lean into it more. "You wanted to stay here, right?"

I nodded, completely shell-shocked.

He'd defended me to the Warden?

But why?

What did he even get out of that?

I was one less number to worry about if I was gone.

Holy shit, I owed this man my damn life.

Or at the very least, some kind of favor.

Was that why he'd done it?

To get something out of me?

I couldn't imagine what the fuck he'd want from an inmate who had nothing to give. I didn't have any money and I certainly didn't have any pull with any of the local gangs.

I was essentially useless to him.

So then, why?

"I want you to finish out this program," Jackson went on. "I think it'll be good for you. Maybe you don't agree with me but that's the way I see it. This program isn't about toughening people up or teaching them to learn a bunch of useless facts about fire fighting. It's about finding the piece inside of you that is dedicated to helping people. I may not know you, Ayen, but I can tell that you can understand that."

I swallowed thickly.

Even though Jackson would never know it, his words meant a lot to me.

Up until the day I'd gotten arrested, I'd been considered a wallflower, a shy and naive boy who never knew what he wanted out of life. There wasn't a day that passed by where I didn't feel like I was in the way or that I was a burden to someone.

Especially my ex.

Even now, two years later, it hurt to think about.

All those nights I'd spent trying to convince him that I wasn't meant to be some house husband who stayed in line and did whatever he wanted—I had dreams and passions, too, and just because I didn't know what they were or where I wanted to go with them, didn't mean that they weren't *real.*

Hearing Jackson talk about something like that had the memories of my past flooding back into my mind, reminding me of the person I'd always been dying to be but never got a chance to because the justice system was fucking rigged. No one cared about a kid who was barely legal at the time being manipulated for years on end to the point of snapping and doing something that could never be taken back.

All anyone saw of me now was a cold-blooded murderer. Not the abused husband who'd been trying to run away only to get caught in the end.

But not Jackson.

He saw the *real* me.

Or at least until he found out about what I'd been sent to prison for. I was sure after that, he'd change his tune real fast.

Most people did, but then again, could I really blame them?

Until then though, I'd bask in his confidence in me.

"Thank you," I said quietly.

He smiled and slowly let go of me. "Did you want something to eat? I made pancakes. They're probably not as good as the ones down at the mess hall, but they do the job."

My skin burned where he'd touched. The remnants of the heat of his hand on me felt like a brand that I never wanted to fade. I liked how it felt, him touching me so casually and like we'd been doing this for a while.

I swallowed again and nodded, taking a seat in one of the chairs at his small dining table, Roxy following me over to join me.

I watched the muscles in his back move as he grabbed the pan and jiggled the pancakes out onto a plate, giving me a nice show on how strong he really was underneath all of that firefighting gear. Even without him being shirtless like that, I knew he was built. But seeing him without anything covering the stark contrasts of his muscles had me wanting to reach out and touch them.

He was certainly strong enough to throw me, all one hundred and thirty pounds, over his shoulder like I was nothing.

"Syrup?" he asked, while opening the fridge.

"Sure, thank you."

He hip-checked it shut before walking over to me with the plates, the bottle of thick syrup tucked under his arm.

The smell was divine as the plate was set down in front of me. He drizzled a nice helping of syrup over my pancakes before moving it over to his and doing the same. A set of silverware was already laid out nicely on a cloth napkin next to me.

"Thank you... for everything, Mr. Hall." I spoke quietly, not at all surprised when Roxy nuzzled her face onto my thigh.

He chuckled. "Please, call me Jax."

CHAPTER NINE

Ayen

BY THE TIME I made it back to my cabin, it was well after roll call and the beginning of the third day of our training.

Jackson, or rather *Jax*, had left soon after breakfast and walked me back to my cabin where one of my COs, Barlow, was waiting for me.

"You've got this cabin to yourself for the time being, Gonzalez. *Don't* make me regret that decision."

I nodded to him before ducking inside to change into my uniform for the day.

I hated that Tyson had been sent back to SAC and I hadn't. He'd only acted out of self-defense and yet, he had been punished just the same as the two who'd started the altercation.

He was the one who had been looking forward to this work program since signups were posted. He'd talked *me* into coming along and yet here I was, the one who got to stay while he was shipped back.

It didn't seem fair. Not when Tyson was a good guy who only wanted to do the right thing at the end of the day. He had a hot temper but only when it was triggered. I'd never quite asked him what he'd been sentenced for, but from the stories he'd told me, it had something to do with drug peddling for one of the local cartels.

Petty shit that a kid his age, sixteen at the time of his sentencing, didn't need to be caught up in, let alone serve a ridiculously long sentence for.

As sad as my sentencing had been, my five years was nothing in comparison to his eighteen. By the time he'd get back out onto the streets, he'd be well into his thirties. I had no doubt that he'd make something of himself, but waiting until that could happen had to be torture.

Thankfully, it was never too late to turn your life around with a drug charge on your record. People dealt with that kind of shit all the time.

Mine was a different story, but that was something future me would get to deal with. For now, I simply needed to keep my head down and continue surviving. Three more years and I would be up for parole.

By the time I got changed and out the door again, Barlow already had an impatient frown etched into his face.

Wordlessly, he led me back to the training grounds where there was a demonstration already going on. I sat on one of the stumps in the back, keeping to myself while I tried to concentrate on what was going on.

I hated that feeling of being alone. Without Tyson around to buffer my social awkwardness, I was going to be doing a lot of shit by myself for the next six weeks. And while in hindsight it wasn't as bad as being thrown in the hole for misbehaving when I got back to the prison, I was also going to heavily miss the companionship.

I knew most of the others in this program but we weren't friendly. Not like Tyson and I were.

Whatever. I was a grown ass adult. I needed to get my act together and stop being upset that I no longer had a friend to hang out with. This program was meant to look good on my record and hopefully, get the parole board to give me a lighter parole sentence once I got out.

I was already looking at a minimum of a year being monitored.

Hopefully, that would be it, though.

A shadow suddenly loomed over me, causing my entire body to tense. I waited, feeling the person behind me hovering closely and hoping they'd pass by soon. When nothing moved, I forced myself to look up.

Jackson was standing right by my stump with Roxy lying down at his feet, her head resting on top of one of his shoes. His arms were crossed over his large chest while he watched the demo ahead of us, a blank expression on his face.

I forced myself not to grin at him and instead, turned back to the demo just as one of my fellow inmates was called up as a volunteer to shoot off a fire extinguisher at one of the blazing fire pits.

For some reason, having Jackson at my back felt comfortable.

Safe even.

Such a difference in how it'd been with my ex. I'd lived in constant fear of that man and what he would do to me if I so much as sneezed wrong. For our entire almost ten year relationship, I'd walked on eggshells. I never knew what would make him flip and go nasty. I often felt like his moods were on a light switch and with one quick flick he'd go from loving and nice to mean and abusive. It was emotionally and mentally draining, that's for sure, but that was no real excuse for what I'd done.

In a way, I was sad for what had transpired between us in the end. No one deserved to be left in the state the bullet had left him in after it'd lodged itself into the left side of his temporal lobe, effectively robbing him of everything but the shell of his former self.

But as fucked up and selfish as it was to think about, I wouldn't take it back. Because in that moment, at the very end of it all, my survival instincts finally kicked in and it was either him or me.

And I chose me.

Probably for the first time in my life.

Jackson unfolded his arms and began to clap, pulling me out of my thoughts while the rest of our group erupted into a smattering of claps to mimic his. One of the volunteer firemen took back the extinguisher once more and thanked his participant before dismissing him back to his stump.

"You want to go up there next?" Jackson whispered at me, his face suddenly twisting into an amused smile.

"You'd have to drag me up there by my hair," I quipped back, not thinking twice.

He only chuckled but didn't push any further. "I'll keep that in mind for next time."

A shiver rolled up my spine.

His words almost sounded like a promise.

A promise I almost wanted him to follow through with.

CHAPTER TEN

Ayen

THE BAG THAT was strapped to my back was heavy, weighing me down as we trekked through the forest. The vegetation wasn't particularly dense but with all of us in heavy protective gear and lugging the bags around, it made for a difficult walk.

After the demonstration of putting out a fire with hand-held intervention, gear had been distributed amongst all of us for a day-long hike into the woods where we'd be shown different burn sites and how to go about spotting the signs of what would constitute a controlled burn and what wouldn't.

I had to say, I was actually pretty interested in learning all of this. Never in my life did I think I'd ever care about forest fires or helping to control or stop them, but with Jackson's words still ringing in my ear from this morning, it had me feeling inspired.

Maybe that was the point of his speech to me—to get me thinking about doing something with my life after I got out, something important that would give back to my community in some way. Maybe he was just being nice and wanted to help a kid like me out because that was kind of his job and there was nothing deeper to it.

Regardless of what his motives were for reassuring me this morning, I still wanted to make him proud.

I sucked the fresh mountain air into my lungs, breathing deeply; it felt nice to be out here in the open again.

Having been locked up for so long and only getting an hour of rec time every day was demoralizing and always had me feeling restless like I was in some kind of perpetual hamster cage.

I understood that going to prison was punishment and that punishment wasn't supposed to be comfortable. Doing penance for my sins wasn't supposed to be some walk in the park where I got to just hang around for five years in some cushy cell while my ex's family had to take care of what was, essentially, a thirty-nine-year-old adult baby for the rest of their lives.

But damn did it feel nice to finally be free for a little while.

I felt something brush against my leg and turned to look down at it, spotting Roxy happily trotting along next to me. I smiled and looked toward the back of the group where Jackson was taking up the rear.

He was engaged in a deep conversation with Barlow, who was visibly sweating from our hike. My CO was nodding along to whatever Jackson was saying while he was fixing his eyes down at the ground with a strained frown.

Clearly this hike wasn't on his list of things he wanted to be forced into doing—especially with his heavy uniform on.

I turned back ahead to face the rest of

the group, ignoring the subtle feeling of eyes on the back of my head.

I was probably blowing it out of proportion, but would it be wrong of me to assume Jackson sent Roxy up here with me to keep me company?

I was the only one out of the group not walking next to someone, after all.

I brushed my hand against her head as we walked, petting her every so often as I whispered how much of a good girl she was. She seemed happy to accompany me, her tail swaying behind her while she navigated the slightly rocky terrain with ease.

Eventually, we reached a large set of stones that looked to be carved down intentionally, giving most of us a spot to rest while we took a water break. I claimed one of the smaller rocks toward the far right side and set my bag between my legs. The zipper parted easily as I peeled it open, trail rations and my thermos of water were right on top. I tossed some of my jerky to Roxy after ripping open the bag, belatedly realizing that I probably should've asked Jackson first before doing that. I winced.

With my luck, his dog was on some super fancy diet that only contained fresh cooked ingredients from a local butcher shop.

"How we doing over here?"

I looked up mid-chew to Jackson coming over to us. Roxy let out a few barks and circled around her owner's legs, before coming back over to me.

"Good. Hey, listen... your dog isn't on a special diet or anything right?"

He laughed. "Uh oh. Did she manage

to weasel something out of you?"

I looked down guiltily at my pack of jerky. "Uh..."

"I swear it's the eyes," he said, flashing me a smile and bending down to grab his dog and ruffle her fur. "She'll get you to give her anything with the right look."

I smiled a little and shoved another slice into my mouth. He wasn't mad, that was a good sign. I hadn't realized how much my heart rate had spiked when he'd come over until I was starting to feel my body relax again.

Jesus, who knew PTSD was such a bitch?

"You got enough water?" He nodded to my bag.

"Yeah. I'm all good. Did *you* drink anything yet?"

"Hey now, I'm the one that's supposed

to be taking care of you. Not the other way around."

You, he said.

Not *you guys,* as in the whole group of us.

Why did that small, subtle word feel like it had something else behind it—like it was charged with more than just him looking out for me because I was technically under the program's care?

Jackson had a way of saying things rather flippantly, even with the underlying message sounding so much more than what was being said on the surface level. I was the king of over-thinking everything, too, that much I was conscious of.

But then, why was I getting the feeling that he was purposefully not looking at me now?

Instead, he was focused on rubbing

Roxy's belly as she rolled around on the ground, getting her golden fur dirty with bits of dead leaves and dirt.

"Well, you've done a good job so far," I said, shoving another piece of jerky into my mouth.

His head snapped up to look at me, freezing me in my place.

Something passed through his eyes, causing my stomach to clench with excitement. I doubted he was trying to give me what I could only describe as bedroom eyes, yet the intense focus was making me squirm.

Shit, I really did over-think all of this, didn't I?

Jackson rose to his feet and stepped around his dog, coming closer to me.

My gaze tracked his every movement, my heart picking up its thrumming beat again as he slowly squatted down in front of me and, without warning, gently cupped one of my legs.

His fingers worked quickly at the laces of my boot, gently pulling it off of my foot and setting it down next to the rock I was sitting on. He rested my heel against his thigh and pushed the cuff of my pant leg up just enough to expose my ankle to him.

I swallowed, his fingers brushing over the skin right above where my sock was and trailing down to my ankle bone. He eased pressure into the tendon, running his fingers up and around a few times while tingles spread throughout my entire leg.

I let out a little groan of pleasure and tightened both of my hands around the pack of jerky as I stayed very still, not wanting to break the moment—wherever the hell it was leading to.

Around us, our group was already beginning to pack up, our break over with.

"Hey, what's going on with him?" The crunch of Barlow's boots were making their way over here.

"Looks like he twisted his ankle," came Jackson's easy reply.

Glee shot through me almost instantly.

Jackson's eyes flitted up to find mine again, searching me for any kind of objection while he continued to massage my lower calf and ankle. He wouldn't find one, though, because there was no way in hell I was breaking up this moment.

"Jesus fuck, Gonzalez," Barlow grumbled. "Are you the clumsiest motherfucker on this planet, or what?"

"Guess so, sir," I said, ripping my gaze away from the man in front of me to focus on my CO instead.

He sighed. "You need to go back to medical?"

"I think he'll be all right with a little more rest," Jackson said, leaning back to show Barlow my ankle. "The swelling's already coming down. Elevating it for another forty-five minutes should do the trick."

Barlow grunted. "We don't have forty-five fucking minutes, Hall."

Jackson made a show of glancing back toward the rest of the group, a frown on his face. My leg involuntarily twitched in Jackson's hold, causing him to tighten his hands around it to secure me.

Thank fuck that I decided to put my rations pack on my lap or else I'd blow my cover with how turned on this entire interaction was making me.

"Why don't you all go on ahead? We should be able to catch up by the time you reach the first site." Jackson's head swiveled back around to Barlow again.

"He can't walk on it at all?"

"Not if you want this sprain to turn into a strain."

Barlow grunted.

"It's that or I carry him back to medical," Jackson went on. "Either way, he can't be on it right now."

"Shit..." Barlow mumbled.

The man dragged a tired hand over his jaw, scratching at the stubble forming there. He looked back out across the group to where the three other firefighters and several convicts were standing together in a small group, their packs already on.

There were no other COs that decided to come on our hike together, choosing to voluntarily stay behind once they were told how far we'd be going today. I had a feeling that Barlow drew up short in their lotto and hadn't actually wanted to come with us, but rather *had to* and he was now regretting that choice.

"You think he'll only need forty-five minutes?"

Jackson nodded. "Should be about that. I've got an ice pack in my bag I'll slap on and see how we do with that."

Barlow nodded, dropping his hand from his face. "All right. I'll radio you when we get to the site to see where you're at. If you do have to head back, you need to let me know."

Jackson's thumb stroked along the

edge of my sock, sending small pulses of pleasure right to my groin. "Of course."

As my CO stepped away and headed back to the group, I let myself relax again.

Trying not to read into Jackson keeping me back just yet, I slowly sealed my rations back up and stuffed everything into my pack again but kept it on my lap. Roxy perked up once the group started to file out of our resting area and head down the path again, leaving Jackson and I behind.

"Forty-five minutes, huh," I said as soon as we were completely alone.

He turned back to smile at me, a rather smug look on his face. "Technically, the protocol is half an hour, but what's an extra fifteen?"

My stomach clenched with excitement. Both of us knew that this bogus excuse was, well, bogus.

So why was Jackson leaning into it?

I wasn't going to complain about spending more time with him, though, and maybe our situation from last night and into this morning had left more of a lasting impression on him than I thought.

All of this was fun and games, though. It wasn't serious—it couldn't be. Not with me being actual government property.

"How's it looking, Doc?" I rolled my foot in his hold. "You think I need to take it easy for the rest of the day?"

He chuckled and patted my leg before pulling the cuff of my pant leg down again. "I think you'll live. Just barely, though."

After getting my shoe back on and laced up, he grabbed me by the arm and hoisted me up off the rock. Without even having to ask, he slipped my bag over his shoulder and nodded for me to follow him.

Thankfully, by now, my body had calmed down somewhat, though I was still buzzing from our close proximity.

We walked at a slow pace; much slower than what we had been when we were with the rest of the group. I didn't mind, though. Not if it meant stealing a little time with Jackson without the watchful eyes of my COs around.

Roxy fell in line next to me, keeping up pace with me easily.

"I'm surprised she likes you so much," Jackson said after minute

"Does she usually get scared of inmates?"

He hummed thoughtfully before answering. "Not exactly. She typically keeps her distance but that's not due to any kind of past experiences or anything."

"Oh."

For some reason, that made me feel special. Like I'd been chosen out of the however many dozens of inmates who had come through this program before me.

None had been trusted before this, so what made me so different?

Almost as if reading my mind, Jackson spoke again. "I think it's your soft nature."

My face flushed.

Soft.

If only he knew what I'd been sentenced for—I doubt he'd think of me as 'soft' then.

Holding that gun in my hand, though, the one my ex-husband had bought only a few months prior as a tool to intimidate me with, and pointing it at him, had felt powerful then—holding a tool that could take a life with the simple pull of a trigger was both exhilarating as it was terrifying.

I knew it made me a fucked up monster to think that way, but it was the truth.

That had been the only time in my life that I had ever felt in control of anything.

In prison, I'd been mandated to take a bunch of psych evals and see a counselor regularly to work through and process what had happened. And while I'd told them over and over again that I was sorry and that I regretted my choices, deep down I wasn't.

I never would be.

Perhaps that feeling would go away in time when I got out and started to live my life the way *I* wanted to, but who knew.

Not many people could come back from attempting to kill someone. It fundamentally changes you as a person, no matter what the intentions were behind the action. Deciding to take a life was a crossroads that very few chose to take, and the suffering that followed, those haunting dreams that still kept me up sometimes, were my cross to bear.

"Hey..." A hand on my arm stopped me from walking. "Where did you go?"

"Huh?" I glanced up at Jackson, confused.

He was frowning down at me. "You disappeared... You did that yesterday, too."

Disappeared?

"I did?"

Looking around the trail, I didn't see any footprints from my boots that told me

I'd wandered off the path. We were still on the same trail and walking at the same casual pace we had been.

"Yeah..." Jackson turned to face me fully, his hand coming up to cup my jaw. Using his other hand, he tapped lightly on my forehead. "Up here. You went somewhere."

My eyes widened.

Oh.

How the hell could he tell that?

I wasn't saying anything out loud, nor was I distracted in my thoughts for that long. Either he'd been watching me the whole time, or I'd somehow made it obvious my mind had drifted away from our conversation.

"Oh. Sorry."

"What were you thinking about?"

Being there in the middle of the woods

alone with him was doing some fucked up things to me. I wanted to stay like this, with him touching me and keeping me close like I was something precious to him. But at the same time, I was petrified that we were going to get caught.

How would this look to anyone, especially a CO, passing by?

I'd be dragged back to SAC faster than I could blink and probably thrown in the hole until my parole hearing.

Hell, Jackson would definitely lose his job, too, if people thought he was fraternizing with the inmates.

"Nothing," I said quickly. "Just about what you said this morning."

His brows pulled together for a moment as he tried to recall our conversation. Whatever he remembered had his expression softening, though, and he reached out, moving his thumb over my cheek like it had this morning.

I wanted to lean into it so bad, nuzzle my face into his hand while he continued to touch me.

"It's the truth, Ayen. You deserve to find yourself while you're here, or whatever truth you're searching for at least."

My lips parted, though I had nothing to really say to that.

His belief in me to change, or rather, become a different person than the one who was caught and thrown into prison, was touching. Back home, I didn't have anyone. Not a mom or dad or any siblings who were eagerly waiting for me to get released.

That was what had made me so susceptible to my ex's attention. I basked in it, reveled in it, even, because it was the first time in my life that I truly felt wanted.

Hearing all of this was addictive.

Could I believe Jackson?

Did I want to?

I'd trusted my ex in much the same way and look where that had gotten me.

But this man was so much different than Alex. He was compassionate and dedicated with his work and with the inmates that were here, and he took the time to check in on me, even without me asking for it.

"I want to trust you," I whispered.

His lip quirked up into a smile. "You can."

My breath hitched as he leaned forward, his gaze darting down to focus on my lips.

CHAPTER ELEVEN

Jackson

AYEN WAS STILL as I leaned forward to kiss him, his cheeks pink with a light flush while my impulsive desires took over and drove me into pulling him closer to me.

His lashes fluttered down over those beautiful brown eyes of his, hiding them from me. I longed to stare into them again and watch his pupils dilate like they had right before he'd closed them on me but held off on asking him to open them again.

Instead, I tilted my head and brushed my lips over his.

They were just as soft as I thought they'd be, pursed enough for me to deepen my peck into an actual kiss.

He let out a small, barely audible noise from his throat that had me wanting to back him up into the nearest tree immediately.

Fuck, I wanted him.

I'd never wanted someone this badly in my life. We had a good twenty-five minutes until I needed to check back in with the group. That was plenty of time to get Ayen undressed enough to touch him and to feel the rest of him to see if his body matched these perfect lips of his.

The radio at my hip screeched loudly, jerking us both apart.

"*Fuck.*" I ripped it off of my belt and flipped to the channel it was signaling me to go to. "What?"

"Mr. Hall," CO Barlow's voice crackled over the frequency. "How's Gonzalez's ankle doing?"

I held back rolling my eyes.

Barlow struck me as an overbearing watchdog that didn't know when to trust the authority of those around him. He was constantly double-checking my and my team's work, even with our track record being as stellar as it was.

It had me wondering what the hell he was like back in the prison and in his element—I'm sure he was known for running a tight ship but translating that into the outside world with a work program was never a good fit.

To do this kind of job, flexibility to the unplannable was your best bet.

"He's doing fine." Ayen quickly averted his eyes while I spoke, clearly flustered with what just happened. But he didn't step away from me or put any distance between us. In fact, he'd practically tucked himself against me. "We'll be meeting up with you all in a bit."

"Make it quick. We're almost at the site."

"Sure. Will do." As I flipped back to the main channel, I sighed.

The atmosphere was awkward now and still filled with that unresolved tension that had been brewing between us since this morning. I'd been trying to convince myself that I was reading into it, seeing signs that weren't really there when it came to Ayen and his sweet attitude.

But he continued to play with me—bantering back and forth—and had not at all leaned away from me as I pressed at those boundaries that separated inmate from volunteer.

He'd whole-heartedly leaned into them with me.

"I, uh..." Ayen cleared his throat. "I guess we should get going then."

I frowned.

Fuck, maybe I really *was* reading way too much into all of this. He could just be placating me because I was the only familiar face around now that his friend was gone.

Guilt curled in my stomach. "Yeah, of course."

I waved him on and began walking,

silence falling over us the entire way there.

CHAPTER TWELVE

Jackson

WE AVOIDED EACH other for the rest of the day—or rather, I kept my distance.

I couldn't bear to look at Ayen if it turned out I really had misstepped and crossed over a major boundary and he now hated me for it. I wouldn't blame him, as I would obviously feel the same in his shoes. To have someone you trusted pressure you into something...

Fuck.

My head was an entire mess, toggling between replaying exactly what happened and filling in the blanks of what 'could've been'.

The noise he'd made had been enticing, but it wasn't like I could judge anything off of just that.

He hadn't leaned away from me or fought me off, but what if he'd simply been scared?

I had no idea what his past was like, and aside from that small glimpse the night I'd pulled him out of his cabin after that fight, I couldn't exactly claim to know anything.

The more time I spent with Ayen, the more I wanted to get to know him. He had a deep inner world that I was desperate to learn about, especially when he got caught up in whatever memory or thoughts that took him out of our conversation for a time.

In all my years of doing this program, not once did I ever think about looking into an inmate's rap sheet. Yet, as soon as we'd all gotten back from our hike and the inmates had been sent to the mess hall for dinner, I was pulling up a chair at the COs table.

"You look like shit," one of the other COs said to Barlow once he slid into a chair at the table with a tray full of food.

"You try walking in eighty degree fucking heat with this fucking uniform," the man grumbled back, digging his fork through a scoop of corn.

"How's Gonzalez's foot, Hall?" one of the COs, Stinner, I think his name was, asked. "Heard he was hobbling around all afternoon."

I paused with my fork at my mouth as I tried to think of some excuse.

"He's probably faking it," Browne chimed in. "Remember what he was like when he first got put onto the unit?"

The entire table erupted into laughter, which made my blood boil.

But I could either sit there and be mad at them for talking shit, or I could use this to my advantage and dig up some info out of them on the man who was beginning to haunt my every thought.

"Why? What was he like?" I asked.

Browne scoffed. "He acted like this scared little puppy. Always trying to get sent to the infirmary for... what the fuck was his excuse?"

"Panic attacks," Stinner volunteered.

Browne jabbed his fork in the direction

of his coworker, nodding. "Yeah. That shit. Funny considering he's a *hot one.* So I don't know why the fuck he was trying to play the baby bird card."

My brows shot up practically into my hairline. "Pardon?"

Stinner leaned over toward me. "He's got a body on his rap."

"Stop talking, both of you," Barlow snapped. "Hall, you keep that shit to yourself or we're all fucked up the ass by the state."

I ripped my gaze away from the group in order to scan through the entire mess hall, searching for him—my so-called baby bird. It took me a minute to find him tucked into the corner away from everyone else, where he ate quietly by himself.

Was that why everyone stayed away

from him?

Because they were scared?

But they're all non-violent.

For some reason, remembering that eased me.

Ayen wasn't violent, of course he wasn't. He was the furthest thing from it. Murdering someone was serious, but to be in this program, it had to be either a complete accident or for a good reason. He wouldn't have been let out of SAC otherwise.

How long was his sentence, anyway?

That'd give me a good indication on what kind of charge it was.

Underneath the table, my leg began to bounce.

"Hall, you hear me?" Barlow said.

"Yeah, no worries. I'm not all that interested in his background," I lied. "I'm here to make sure they all walk out of this program still alive."

Stinner laughed. "Close call the other night with that fight?"

"Where the fuck did they swipe the cards from, anyway?" Browne asked.

"Who knows and who fucking cares."

My mind wandered as their conversation deviated from Ayen. My heart squeezed; watching him eating alone by himself as he hunched over his food had me fighting the urge to go over there and claim a spot at his table. His gaze was moving slowly around the hall, taking in the other inmates around him, until he caught sight of me watching him.

A small, quick, smile was flashed my way before he looked back down at his food again.

My entire body relaxed at the sight of

it.

Was I forgiven for earlier?

Without any hesitation, my mind was made up. I had to know.

Later tonight, after lights out, I'd sneak over to his cabin to talk to him about what happened during our hike.

I had to make sure we were still good or else it was going to kill me.

CHAPTER THIRTEEN

Jackson

IT WASN'T HARD to sneak out from my cabin and over to the inmates' after lights out.

Not many firefighters were eager to be moving around the dark property this late at night unless they were coming back from the city, and as far as I knew, no one had taken off for a night at the bars.

With only one CO on watch for the

night, the rest were asleep in their cabins, making it easy for me to avoid the view of the cameras as I reached Ayen's cabin.

The door was unlocked, unsurprisingly, and opened with barely a creak as I slipped inside. Outside, the world was silent, only broken up by the occasional chirping of a cricket nearby.

Fishing my phone out of my pocket, I unlocked it and shined the light down at the floor.

"Ayen," I whispered into the dark.

A figure shot up from the bottom right bunk immediately, kicking back until he was pressed flat against the wall. The sound of panicked breathing broke up the silence in the cabin, filling it with an anxious tension.

I kept the light tilted down so that it didn't flash in the window and catch the attention of whoever was manning cameras as I walked over to the bed. "It's just me."

"Jax?" He sounded terrified.

Poor baby.

"Yeah."

There was the slow sound of him letting out a long and barely controlled breath, the gasp and hitch in his throat at the tail end of it, had my heart sinking in my chest.

A sigh left him as his silhouette finally relaxed. "What are you doing here?"

I wanted to pull him up from his bed and hold him against my chest until he finally relaxed again. The urge burned as I ignored it. "I wanted to talk to you without all the COs around."

He was quiet when I sat down at the end of his bed. His legs were drawn up to his chest protectively, his arms wrapped around them in a tight hold.

I wanted to reach out and touch him, pull him away from the corner he'd squished himself into. This was the second time I'd seen him have this kind of reaction—to immediately shrink away from whatever perceived danger he thought he was in and try to hide.

My hand tightened around my phone.

I wanted to find the motherfucker who had hurt him enough to illicit that kind of response and show them what *real* fear was like.

"Everything okay?" he asked.

His eyes reflected in my phone's light as I slid it face down toward the wall so that the light bounced off the bottom of the top bunk and cocooned us in the soft glow. He was watching me curiously, no hint of being scared or upset at all reflected back at me.

"I think so." I hooked my leg up over my knee. "I hope so."

"Is Roxy okay?"

I smiled. "Yeah, she's all good."

Ayen slowly stretched his legs out in front of him. He scooted across the small twin mattress in order to come closer to me, swinging his legs over the side of the bed. We were only a few inches apart now, enough where I could feel the heat of his body refracting off of him.

"Is this about earlier?" His eyes were drawn to the floor.

Shit.

"Yes." My throat was tight as I said the word.

Don't get me wrong, I'd been rejected plenty of times in my forty-five years on this Earth. I'd always taken it in stride and never once thought badly of the other person who was doing the rejecting. That was simply a fact of life and one that I accepted wholeheartedly.

This felt worse for some reason, though. Like I was suddenly back in high school and getting turned down by my first crush.

"I'm sorry," he mumbled.

Incredulously, I asked, "What are *you* sorry for?"

"I..." His shoulders sagged inward, practically pinching up against his ears. "I got you in trouble, didn't I?"

"Why would you think that?"

He glanced at me. "Isn't that why you were sitting with the COs?"

I couldn't help it, I burst out laughing. "No, of course not."

Was it better if I was honest with him about what my intentions were with sitting with the COs?

Or did I hold off on that for now and steer our conversation elsewhere?

It might freak him out if he thought I was fishing for more info on his background, especially with a murder charge tacked onto him.

"I wanted to talk about earlier, too." I moved again, hooking my right leg up onto the mattress in order to face him fully. Not being able to help myself and because I was clearly half a masochist, I reached out and grabbed at the hands resting in his lap. "How did you feel about what happened earlier?"

"I liked it," he whispered.

My heart raced in my chest. "Do you want to do it again?"

My voice had dropped low, thick with want for him. I could already feel my cock growing hard in my pants and had to force myself to remain still until Ayen answered me. I *needed* his truth—to know I wasn't the only one feeling this insane spark between us.

"Yes." He swallowed hard enough that his Adam's apple bobbed. "D... Do you?"

"Absolutely." I let go of one of his hands and cupped his face, pulling him closer to me. "Tell me to stop if you need me to."

He shook his head in my hand, his tongue darting out to wet his bottom lip.

I yanked him in for another kiss, this time not holding back like I had in the forest. Here, no one was around to interrupt us, or catch us in the act. I could savor the taste of him, memorize every part of him as much as he let me.

Ayen exhaled out a small noise when I swiped my tongue against the seam of his mouth, beckoning him to open it for me and let me in. He only hesitated for a second before he was parting his lips, allowing me to deepen our kiss.

He was shy when his tongue met mine, gently pressing it along the side while I rolled mine around, tasting every inch of him like I'd been dying to for the past few days. He moaned again and leaned his body toward mine, one of his hands coming up to grasp at the front of my shirt.

My cock strained at the front of my pants, begging to be let out. From just a kiss, I was already getting this turned on.

What the hell was this man doing to me?

Without breaking our mouths apart, I snaked a hand around Ayen's back and hooked it low enough to bend him backward and lay him down onto the bed. He let out a small gasp when our bodies pressed up against each other.

His cock was hard against my hip, small and cute, just like he was. I was dying to see and touch it, to feel how lost it would get in my large hand while I let him fuck himself inside my fist.

How much cum would he spill as he reached his climax?

What kind of expression would his face twist into right before he came?

"I want to touch you," I told him, breaking our kiss while a thin trail of spit kept us linked for a second longer. "Will you let me?"

He nodded quickly, already lost in

what we were doing.

I loved how riled up he could get so easily.

Normally, in situations like this, I wanted to take my time. I liked to savor the moments before the actual act, watching my sub squirm and beg while I teased them until they cried. I wouldn't be able to get that far with Ayen, not with him looking already fucked out of his mind with just a simple kiss.

He was wearing a pair of cotton pants that were doing nothing to hide his arousal. I tugged at the drawstring until it came loose, and then hooked both sets of my fingers under the band and scooted the material down his hips. He popped free of the garment easily, his cute little pink cock already wet at the tip as it rested against his stomach.

"Um, Jax..." His expression suddenly grew worried, his gaze darting over to the door to the cabin.

"Don't worry, baby. I got you." I rubbed a hand up and down his side a few times. "We'll be quiet."

He trusted me; he said so himself that morning. I wouldn't let him down with that. As much as I wanted to get lost in him and let us both drown in this pleasure, I wasn't going to let him get caught and punished. His outcome would be far worse than mine, anyway.

The most that would happen to me was I'd get let go with the heavy disappointment from my chief following me.

Ayen would fare far worse, which I simply couldn't let happen.

Pushing his t-shirt up to his chest, I

pressed a few soft kisses along his sternum and down to his stomach.

That seemed to relax him as he sighed softly and sunk deeper into his mattress. "Okay."

My lips soon found the tip of his cock, my tongue darting out to lap up the pearl of precum that had already leaked out of him. His body jerked at the contact, another gasp leaving his lips.

"Shhh," I rubbed his side again. "Be good for me and cover your mouth, okay?"

He nodded quickly and slapped a hand over his mouth, moaning into it.

So obedient.

I absolutely *loved* that.

Lying down on my stomach with his thighs parted on either side of me, I held his hips down in a tight hold and licked up the length of him. His cock twitched from the contact while his balls drew up toward his shaft, more precum leaking out of him.

Shit, if he was already reacting this much to a few swipes of my tongue, how was he going to handle being in my mouth completely?

"When's the last time someone had you in their mouth, baby?"

He shook his head quickly, the muscles in his stomach flexing.

"*Never?*"

He shook his head again.

I let out a soft 'tsk'. "Well, that's changing tonight."

Honestly, what kind of guys did he date before this for them to deny him like that?

Some Doms were too selfish and didn't deserve to have a beautiful and perfectly little obedient sub like Ayen under them.

If there was no give and take to a relationship then what was the point?

Grabbing his free hand, I brought it up to tangle in my hair. "You tell me if it gets to be too much, okay?"

He nodded once more.

"Good boy," I praised, because he really was.

He groaned against his hand again, clearly liking hearing that.

Without another moment of hesitation, I licked up the length of him again and then slipped his cock head into my mouth. His body jerked instantly, his chest expanding with how quickly he sucked in a breath.

I held him still while I rolled my tongue around his tip, tasting the saltiness of him and teasing that slit that kept insisting on squeezing as much precum out of him as possible.

He moaned against his hand loudly this time, his fingers tightening their hold in my hair, and it drove me absolutely fucking insane.

It was like he couldn't decide on whether he wanted to thrust up into my mouth or just lay back and let me do whatever I wanted to him. Either one I would be fine with in any other normal circumstances, but tonight I wanted to spoil him. He wasn't going to have to work for anything if he wanted it.

I curled my tongue around the underside of him while I slid my mouth down on him more, bobbing up and down a few times to wet the skin as I went. He was a little heavier on my tongue than I expected, but I could wrap my lips around him perfectly.

I wondered how many people had had the pleasure before me to see him like this, naked and begging to be tasted, and never took the opportunity to do so.

What a damn shame.

However, at the same time, I was thankful that I'd be the first one to do this to him.

The memory would be ingrained into his brain for the rest of his life.

As I moved my mouth down until my lips were pressed into the soft curls at his base, he didn't even tickle against the back of my throat, just barely reaching my uvula. I stayed there for a long moment, letting my mouth tighten around him as I swiped my tongue around him a few times.

This felt good—this felt *right*. He was

meant to be here, laying on this bed while he had his cock stuffed into my mouth.

My cock hurt with how hard I was, causing me to grind my hips down into his mattress, aching for some kind of relief. I wanted to bury myself inside of his tight little hole and feel him squeeze around me until he had me coming.

"Jax..." His voice sounded so broken through his fingers.

I pulled off of him immediately and wrapped a hand around him instead. "Does this feel good, Ayen?"

He choked out another quiet moan. "I'm... I'm gonna..."

I grinned, stroking my hand up and down him slowly. "I want you to. I want you to come right in my mouth so I can taste you, honey. You'll do that for me, right? You'll let me have it?"

"Fuck." Ayen's hips rolled forward, practically trying to grind himself up into my hand. He was so pretty like this; the image of him was going to be burned into my mind after this for the rest of the night.

Maybe forever.

I wrapped my lips around his cock head again, massaging my tongue around and under the sensitive tip while my hand did the work in stroking him in a smooth rhythm. His body arched up under me, one of his legs coming around to hook around my back to hold me against him. I let spit dribble down from my mouth to my hand, slicking it up while I continued to stroke up to where my chin was.

"J-Jax—"

He didn't get to finish whatever it was he was trying to say to me, his orgasm taking over and spilling his cum into my mouth. His strangled gasp had me deep-throating him again, getting him all the way back toward my throat so he could empty himself right into my throat. Just as I'd wanted him to.

His hand tightened in my hair hard enough to hurt my scalp, but damn, the pain was worth it to see his twisted up face fall into bliss. He let out a silent scream, his mouth dropping open while his eyes screwed tightly shut.

His body jerked with each spurt of cum he shot down my throat, thick and warm while it slid down into my belly. He held onto me for dear life, letting me help him through until he was finally done and lying completely spent on the mattress.

Beautiful...

So, so beautiful.

The hand in my hair fell down onto the bed next to him uselessly as he panted, his eyes finally opening again while he blinked wordlessly at the bunk above him.

The look on his face had me chuckling as I slowly slid my mouth off of him to sit up, licking my lips to swipe up whatever remnants were left behind.

Delicious.

His cock lay wet on his stomach, a thin sheen of sweat starting to gleam on his skin. Jesus, I wanted to lick at every inch of him, lap at him like a damn cat.

"Jax," he mumbled.

Leaning over, I pressed a soft kiss to his lips.

I wanted to stay, so goddamn badly. But I'd already been here long enough to press my luck. We'd have to continue another day. Now that I had a taste for him, I wasn't going to give him up. I had him in my veins, my addiction already manifesting.

"Be good and get some rest, okay?" I spoke softly. "I'll see you tomorrow."

He nodded at me wordlessly, pursing his lips again for another kiss.

Smiling, I pressed my lips to his once more before climbing off of him and grabbing his pants from where I'd tossed them. They slipped on easily and I was sad to cover up that beautiful little cock of his once more from my view.

He sighed softly when I tucked him in, snuggling down into the thin sheets like they were made of the finest silk.

My feet felt glued to the floor, and I was unable to move as I watched him drift off to sleep.

How bad would it be if I stayed just until the sun came up?

I could sneak out then... run back to my cabin and shower before morning roll call.

Maybe I could even wake up earlier than that and roll Ayen over onto his side and see just how far I could coax my cock inside of him before he woke up.

I gripped myself through my pants.

Shit, I really needed to go *before I actually gave in to my desires*.

It was a chore to force myself to take my phone and leave.

By the time I got back to my cabin, I was already missing him. Roxy whined at me when I finally shut the door behind me, clearly smelling Ayen's scent on me. She obviously missed him just as much as I did.

I crouched beside her to run my hands over her soft coat. "I know, girl. Me too."

CHAPTER FOURTEEN

Ayen

MY EYES SHOT open the moment the sun peered in through the window.

Blearily, I looked around for any signs that last night had happened and it wasn't just some wild dream my brain cooked up because I was horny beyond belief for a man twice my age and who should be staying far, far away from me.

Nothing seemed out of place. The door

was still closed and none of my belongings had been moved around at all.

Grabbing at my sheets, I lifted them to my nose and inhaled deeply. I could smell Jackson but it was barely there, only a faint whiff that could've been left over from spending time with him on our hike.

But it was still there, even if barely.

That spicy scent that I wanted to bury my face in and drown was still embedded in the sheets.

Keeping the sheets pressed up against my nose, I slipped my hand under my pajama pants and fisted my half hard cock. A moan left me instantly as I felt the slight stickiness left over from my cum and his mouth that had been slicked all along my skin.

I stroked myself slowly, remembering every single detail of him going down on me.

I wasn't lying when I said that had been my first time doing something like that. Alex had always been grossed out with giving blowjobs and had only ever wanted to stick his dick into something hot and tight like my ass.

There had been the occasional holiday blowjob that he'd *allowed* me to give him, but it never lasted long until he was pulling me up from my knees and bending me over to stick his dick inside me.

I shuddered at the memories.

To my surprise, though, Jackson had been almost enamored with having his mouth wrapped around me. I didn't have much experience in the sex department but it almost felt like he'd *enjoyed* giving me a blowjob, perhaps even more so than getting off himself.

In fact, I didn't remember him touching himself at all that entire time.

I wondered what his cock looked like. Judging from how far out it'd tented his pants, it was probably huge.

I whined softly, my hand speeding up as my hips rolled to fuck up into it. I wished he didn't have to leave last night, but I understood why he did. I really wished I could've at least reciprocated something and not left him high and dry while I fell asleep content as a damn pillow prince.

Would there be a next time?

I sure as fuck hoped so.

I wasn't going to be satisfied with us only having that one encounter. I needed more of him. Whatever he was willing to give me, I'd take it. I craved it like I craved breathing.

My orgasm spilled out of me, thick cum coating my hand and sticking to my sheet as I glided my cock against it, pretending that it was Jackson's mouth instead.

God, it felt so fucking good coming down his throat.

Collapsing back onto my mattress, I blinked my eyes open again and stared at the bunk above me. Since I was alone in the cabin for the time being, I could probably sneak him back in there tonight.

As long as he was up for it, at least.

Fear curled in my stomach right then, my nature at second-guessing myself rearing its ugly head.

I needed to stop before I talked myself out of it again.

That was what had happened

yesterday back on the hike when I'd tried to pretend like Jackson kissing me was nothing. Because it was anything *but* nothing and yet, I'd gotten too self conscious that he'd feel like he made a huge mistake and regretted it so I'd covered the awkward tension for him by pretending like nothing happened and plowing right on to our task.

I'd been feeling sick to my stomach by the time we'd caught up with the rest of the group and could barely function when he started to completely avoid me. And that was when I'd figured that he really had regretted the kiss.

But last night had proved otherwise.

Smiling to myself, I kicked off my sheets and wandered to the small bathroom to clean myself up.

I didn't know what I was going to do to

get him alone in order to invite him back here tonight, but there had to be some way to slip him a private contact.

A note maybe?

That might be found though and used as evidence against us.

Today, we were going on another hike to more burn sights, one that had already had a controlled burn and they were now reinvigorating the soil nutrients. Maybe after our hike I could catch up with him and talk to him.

Hopefully, we would still be on the same page by then.

CHAPTER FIFTEEN

Ayen

"ALL RIGHT, SPLIT up into groups of two," one of the volunteer firefighters, Mac, as I remembered from our first day, called out to us. "We're going to be doing some surveying while we're out here and gathering test samples for the quality of the soil to send back to one of the labs we work with. We want to make sure that the soil has been properly enriched after our burn and it's reading in the reports."

Our group began to separate themselves into teams, dividing amongst themselves with little hassle. I stood still, rubbing my fingers together at my sides while people moved around me, easily finding their partner and heading over to the tool kits with sample vials in them.

Fuck, this was like getting picked last for teams in high school gym class all over again.

With only twenty-one of us left, I'd be the odd man out and would need to add myself as a third to someone's group.

But who?

A hand at my back pressed against me, gently motioning me forward.

Looking over my shoulder, I spotted Jackson, who nodded toward the tool kits.

"Go on, grab one."

That was the first time I was seeing him since last night. His expression didn't betray anything but his hand sure did, gently tracing along my lower back in small circles where no one could see.

My stomach flipped at the contact while I tried to fight the smile that was trying to work its way onto my face.

I dragged my feet over to the tool kits. There was only one of them left after each of the groups had grabbed theirs. Inside of it were small glass vials, a set of strangely colored liquids, field sheets, and a set of small tools used for digging up dirt.

I hooked it around my waist and tightened the belt until it was snug against me.

Sure, I wasn't exactly thrilled that

Jackson was forcing me to be social, but hopefully, it was only for one day. If I played my cards right, I could potentially mess up one of these tests on purpose and get him to come over to show me, giving me ample opportunity to ask him to stop by later.

"Uh oh."

A hand slapped down on my shoulder. I looked up to see Mac staring down at me.

"No partner, huh?"

"Uh…"

"I'll take him." Roxy trotted over while Jackson followed close behind. "He's still got that ankle thing going on."

"Oh, right. I forgot about that." Mac patted my shoulder. "Keep to the flatter terrain while you're out there, okay? There are a lot of exposed roots since all the undergrowth was burned. We don't need you tripping over something and breaking anything."

I gave him a firm nod. "Of course."

Roxy pressed her wet nose against my palm.

"I'm going to take him down by the river bed," Jackson said. "Less roots down there."

"Good idea." Mac stepped away to attend to another group who was struggling to get their belts on, leaving Jackson and I alone again.

"River bed, huh," I mumbled, making a show at fixing my belt while I could feel my entire face heat up.

"Well, the river's loud this time of year. It will help cover up any screaming."

I choked out a surprised noise and snapped my head up to look at him again.

"Screaming..."

He grinned, shrugging. "I like that you're loud."

Oh. My. God. This man.

"You're a bit full of yourself thinking I'll be screaming your name." My voice was quiet as I spoke. Even as I said the words, though, I knew they were lies. I could barely contain myself last night and it was just a blowjob.

What was going to happen if this progressed into *more*?

I probably *would* be screaming Jackson's name.

He chuckled softly. "Who knows, maybe I'll be screaming yours."

The inside of my cheek hurt from how hard I had to bite it to keep myself from grinning back. Jackson's acceptance of my verbal need was so different than my past with my ex, to the point where it was kind of startling. Alex had hated how noisy I got when I was turned on and always had me pressed down face first into the mattress while he fucked me so it would drown out my moaning.

I'd learned to like it like that, or so I let him believe seeing as how it was the only intimate contact I'd had my entire adult life. If I didn't enjoy it somehow, then it'd feel like a total chore and would be another thing I added to my ever-growing list of things I hated about marriage.

Jackson winked at me before stepping away, heading over to one of the other firefighters to speak with him for a moment. Roxy stayed by my side, sitting down next to me and leaning her body against my thigh to rest.

I stroked her golden fur, luxuriating in

the feel of it under my palm, anticipation racing through me.

A short whistle had both Roxy and I looking over to where Jackson was gesturing. She lifted herself up off the ground and trotted over to him, her tail swishing as she went. Jackson shook the other firefighter's hand before squatting and brushing his hands all over Roxy's face.

She yipped at him as he stood, sticking by the other firefighter's side while Jackson headed back over to me.

"I'm going to have her go with the rest of the group. I don't need her jumping in the water the second we get down there."

"Does she like the water that much?"

He rolled his eyes affectionately. "Oh, you have no idea."

CHAPTER SIXTEEN

Ayen

THE RIVER WAS about half a mile from where the group had set up their temporary test site.

While Jackson and I headed down that way, the rest of the groups fanned out east of us, all of them following the trail of where the controlled burn had begun while we were at the end of it.

The trek down to the edge of the river

was easy, thanks to all of the underbrush having been cleared out and burned back into the soil. The vials inside of my kit clinked softly on my hip as we walked. Jackson and I were close enough that our hands kept brushing together every so often, causing shocks of adrenaline to spike through me.

I was dying to take his hand, but figured crossing that kind of line with him would turn him off. There was a difference between just wanting to fuck someone and doing the lovey-dovey shit.

Jeopardizing whatever this was by getting too ahead of myself would be my biggest regret. So, in order to behave myself, I slipped my hands into my pockets.

"So, where do the samples get sent after we take them?" I asked, the sound of the river growing stronger the farther we walked.

"A lab out in Riverside. They test to see if there's any toxic waste in the soil that'll prevent new growth. We haven't had that happen out here in decades, but we always test just to be safe."

I nodded, interested at the information. "What made you want to do all of this? The wild fire stuff."

"Hmmm." He thought for a moment before answering. "Aside from helping people, I find the taking care of nature part fascinating. There's a lot that goes into it, aside from just the controlled burns and making sure nothing gets out of hand while they're going on. We have to account for burn sites with highly dense populations of certain animal species and taking into account how many deaths will occur and if it's worth the temporary displacement."

"Were you always interested in this sort of thing?"

He laughed. "Actually, no. I was working at a dog rescue before I got involved in any of this with my older brother. That was a long time ago, though."

I smiled. "That's right up your alley."

"You think so?" Jackson brushed his shoulder with mine. "I got tired of it, though. There are so many people that don't know how to properly take care of their dogs. We'd get these poor rescues in that were just a mess. Lot of humane euthanasia. Eventually, it wears on you."

I nodded slowly. "I can see that."

"What about you?" he asked. "What were you doing before the jumpsuit?"

I kind of appreciated that he was being a little more cavalier about my situation—it made me feel less like a pariah. Maybe it wasn't his intention, but it made me feel better nonetheless.

"I, uh... actually didn't have a career."

"No?" His brows pulled together in surprise.

"Yeah... I was actually a stay-at-home husband."

Jackson immediately halted in his tracks, stopping so short that his boots made a divot in the soft soil. "You're married."

Even though whatever we had going on could be seen as highly unethical, I was happy to see he had some morals. Sleeping with a married man was apparently on his list of no-nos, which was partly funny and yet also comforting to me. There were too many people in this world who didn't take their wedding vows seriously enough.

Turning to him, I let out a soft sigh. "I used to be."

"'Used to be'." He shook his head. "What does that mean?"

"Um..."

Jesus, how did I even get into this?

My relationship with Alex was so complicated by the end. I could barely wrap my mind around what happened in order to talk to a therapist about it, let alone right here and now with Jackson.

He waited patiently, though, for me to speak, rubbing his fingers together at his sides in an anxious sort of way.

I wondered if he was seeing me differently. Someone who was once married and now a felon in a program and fucking around with one of the firefighters. See, those things didn't tend to look as bad when you were just dealing with surface level shit. Once people got to know each other, that's when the real mess began to manifest.

I couldn't look him in the eyes as I talked and instead, crossed my arms over my chest while I stared down at the ground. "I, uh... served my ex divorce papers on my twenty-first birthday. I wasn't planning on it being that day but it was the only day I knew he'd be gone for the majority of it so I could pack a bag and leave before he got home and discovered the papers." I huffed out a laugh. "Clearly, that didn't go over very well."

"Why do you say that?"

"Well, he's kind of the reason I got

sentenced. So...”

“*Fuck*, Ayen,” Jackson murmured.

He cupped his hands around my face, tilting it back to force me to look up at him. He was shaking his head, a pinched expression on his face. “He hurt you, didn’t he?”

Over the years, that question had been asked so many times that I’d lost count. Even before my divorce, or my attempt at it, anyway, I’d had friends who would notice my bruises or the bite marks on my skin and ask me if they were from Alex.

And over and over again I’d promised them that it wasn’t him, even when it was obvious and no one believed me, yet they still did nothing to protect me. To help me get out when I needed to.

During my trial, I’d been asked

repeatedly if Alex's stalking had been the cause of me pulling the trigger, or if he'd hurt me the night he came to my apartment, that I thought I'd be safe from him.

I'd been forced to re-live the grim truth, to describe in excruciating detail what transpired on that night.

The fear that choked me as I watched him break down the door to my bathroom, with my phone pressed to my ear and emergency services rattling in my ear about how they were only a few minutes away. The cool steel of Alex's gun that I'd stolen a week earlier resting heavily in my lap, the muzzle of it blurring as I raised it with my shaking hand at the man I once thought I'd loved and pulled the trigger, effectively ending both of our lives in a single split second.

Even after all of that, answering that question never got any easier. No matter how many times how many people asked or how many times I recounted that night.

"Yes," I said, tears burning behind my eyes.

"Oh, honey." Jackson shook his head again, pulling me against him. "He never deserved you."

Shock hit me instantly.

No one had ever said that to me before, let alone meant it.

I was just a runaway kid at sixteen, living off the streets until one day, a man in a suit had found me rifling through his garbage and had invited me to come stay with him for a few days until I could find a shelter that would take me in. Those few days had turned into weeks and then into months, and then soon I was walking down the aisle to marry him.

Alex had made me feel like the luckiest son of a bitch for pulling me off the street like a stray cat and giving me a home like he had. The abuse was simply my burden to bear in order to keep living the life he provided. It was a small price to pay, until it became bad enough where it wasn't so small anymore.

But even then, I thought my karma had earned me that little spot of hell that I called a jail cell.

Yet here Jackson was, telling me the complete opposite with such sincerity that it was hard to peg him as a liar.

I began to shake my head, a knee jerk reaction to the comforting words.

He tightened his hold on my jaw, preventing me from continuing. "Ayen, you listen to me. He. Didn't. Deserve. You.

What you did to him... he fucking deserved that."

"I'm..." My words were failing me. My thoughts were getting all jumbled up in my head as my emotions were beginning to get the better of me. I wasn't expecting to come out here and cry about my past with a man I wanted to rail me into the goddamn dirt like an animal. But here we fucking were. "You don't know..."

"I don't have to know the details, baby. He hurt you. If he hurt you, then he deserved whatever he got in the end." I felt his lips press against the top of my head, peppering kisses into my hair as he spoke.

I sucked in a sharp breath while a sob choked me.

The validation I needed over two years ago had finally been delivered.

It felt as amazing even as it hurt.

I believed wholeheartedly that I would've died that night if I didn't do what I did, but did that justify me taking matters into my own hands?

I still didn't know. But it was too late now to dwell on the 'what if's now.

Jackson pressed his lips to my forehead, trailing soft kisses down to the bridge of my nose. "He can't get you anymore."

My body sagged into his, almost completely boneless.

The truth rattled me to my damn core.

But he was right.

Alex would never hurt or touch me ever again.

CHAPTER SEVENTEEN

Jackson

I LOWERED AYEN to the soft mossy ground slowly, hooking my arm around his waist from behind to keep him from moving too far away from me. My lips found his easily, molding against those soft, plush cushions that he opened for me immediately, sucking me in with the kind of desperation I felt down to my bones.

His cheeks were still wet from his tears, brushing up against mine when he tilted his head to the side to deepen our kiss.

I wanted to kill that son of a bitch he called a husband. If the man wasn't already fucking dead, I'd leave this property tonight and go find him to finish the fucking job.

How dare he put his hands on Ayen?

My sweet baby bird who couldn't even hurt a fly but had apparently been forced to do the worst thing a human could ever possibly do. And the justice system punishing him by forcing him into prison with other offenders who'd knowingly broken the law because they thought they were above it was just the cherry on top of an already fucked up cake.

What kind of 'justice' was that?

And after he got out, he'd have to deal with that on his record for the rest of his life. That sounded like no justice to me.

It infuriated me. I hope that man rotted in fucking hell for the rest of eternity.

Grabbing at the front of Ayen's waistband, I unbuckled the tool kit from around him. The vials inside of it clinked softly as I pushed them away from us so that they wouldn't get damaged. I at least still had some sense about me, even though my mind was filled with *Ayen, Ayen, Ayen.*

I'd show him how to be properly treated—what being with a *real* man felt like. Not some spineless coward who beat their partner because deep down they knew they weren't good enough.

My father was like that. Growing up,

he'd been the stereotypical jock that had wanted his sons to follow in his footsteps and join the military and make something of themselves.

Carter had done that, acted as the proper son that my father should've been proud of. But nothing had ever been good enough for that man. And eventually, it'd weighed on my brother too much for him to bear it any longer.

My brother, and Ayen both, deserved so much better in the end but still had shit to show for it.

When Ayen's legs came up to wrap around my waist, I scooped him up again into my lap and worked the zipped on the front of his jumper down until he could slip both of his arms out of the sleeves. He wrapped his bare arms around my neck while I rolled my tongue along his.

The tent in his pants was pressed up against my waist, teasing me.

Fuck, I needed to get him naked *pronto.*

Keeping him against me with one arm, I used the other to shed my jacket and toss it onto the ground behind him. I laid him back down, keeping him half in my lap with his legs still wrapped around me.

I stroked my hands along his bare skin, touching him and teasing him as I went. Using both of my fingers, I pinched at his nipples, driving a small, surprised squeak out of him that had me chuckling against his mouth.

"Sensitive little thing, aren't you," I said, my voice low and husky. I trailed my lips along his jaw, tracing up to where the shell of his ear was. He shivered again when I nipped at it, taking the lobe into my mouth and flicking it a few times with my tongue.

"Jax," he moaned.

God, I loved the sound of him saying my name like that.

"Want do you want, baby?" I asked, letting go and nuzzling my nose against the side of his face, inhaling his unique scent. I couldn't fucking get enough of him. I need to touch and taste him as much as I needed water to live. "You tell me."

"You." His thighs squeezed around me. "I want you."

That cute little cock of his jerked against my waist, still covered by the bottom half of his jumpsuit. Mine was also dying to get out of my thick trousers and find that soft heat of his that I knew would feel like fucking heaven once I pressed up against it.

"You want all of me?" I asked. I had a feeling, but I needed to be sure. I wasn't going to press him if all he wanted was another blowjob or something low-key, which I'd be more than satisfied to give him.

He nodded, rolling his hips against me. "You have anything on you?"

"Condoms? No. Some kind of lube? I can get creative."

He huffed out a laugh. "I know that wasn't meant to be sexy, but..."

I grinned and lifted myself up from where I'd buried my face in his neck. His smile was a dream, a beautiful change from the absolutely heart-shattered despair that had been on it a few minutes ago. I hated that look on him; it felt too much like angels crying or something equally as biblical.

"Are you okay with that?" I reached over to grab the pack I'd thrown onto the ground the second I'd taken him into my arms. "No protection?"

I slid it back over to me and parted the zipper with one of my hands, my other finding the spot right where Ayen's jumpsuit was still partially zipped and his skin was showing at his hip. He was warm under my hand, solid. I squeezed him, making sure all of this was still real and not some fantasy my mind had cooked up in a dream.

"He was my first," Ayen said, his fingers flexing around my arm. "My only."

I'll be your last, is almost what came spilling out of my mouth in response. Fuck, I really had it bad for him. Not even inside of him yet and I was already hearing the damn wedding bells.

Though, I doubted Ayen would ever want to get married again. Not after what happened with his first husband.

I was getting ahead of myself.

Grabbing the travel-sized bottle of aloe I kept, I shoved my pack away again and set the bottle down next to us. "I'm clean."

He nodded, not even needing me to elaborate further as he said, "I trust you."

My heart thundered in my chest.

The fact that some other man had taken advantage of him killed me. He was so trusting, maybe a little too much so for his own good. And for someone to have taken that and used it to their advantage truly sickened me.

That stopped here. I don't know how I was going to accomplish it but starting now, I wouldn't allow anyone to take him for granted again.

Ayen unhooked his legs from around me, pulling them back just enough to help me lift him and slip the bottom half of his jumpsuit and boots off of his body. He was as beautiful as I remembered him from last night, now fully revealed to me through the breaks of sunlight through the thick canopy over us.

His tanned skin was flawless and smooth, a dusting of hair trailing down to his hard cock that rested against his lower belly, straining to be touched. I fisted my hand around it immediately, not being able to help myself.

Ayen groaned, his back arching. "Ohhhh..."

I stroked my hand down him slowly, lovingly. Beads of precum leaked out from the engorged tip and down to my hand where I spread it along his shaft as I continued to move my hand, working him.

"Jax," his voice was strained. He reached out to grab at the moss-covered ground, fingers clenching tightly around it. "Please..."

My own cock jerked in my pants, completely on board with the begging.

I'd had subs before beg for me to fill them, on their hands and knees as they presented themselves to me like cats in heat. None of them had ever come close to turning me on quite like this. Ayen's unabashed *want* for me was so intoxicating that I was willing to drown on it.

"Hold still," I told him and let go of him.

Standing, I quickly kicked my boots off and yanked my undershirt off, tossing them both toward my pack with little care.

Ayen sat up on his elbows to watch me, his eyes practically bulging out of his head when I shrugged my pants down and stepped out of them.

"Like what you see?" I teased.

His mouth dropped open, his eyes directly narrowing in on my cock.

Its heavy weight bounced while I moved, sinking back down to my knees on the soft moss in front of him and scooting closer so that he could wrap his legs around me again if he wanted to.

"Fuck," he mumbled. "You're fucking huge..."

I chuckled, scooping the bottle of aloe off of the ground. "Oh, he flatters me."

"Um..."

I glanced at him, uncapping the bottle

as he spoke.

"So, the last time I did this was three years ago."

"You'll be okay, Ayen. I won't hurt you." Probably. Good thing I had a ton of aloe in this bottle.

He didn't look convinced in the slightest, and instead of leaning back and parting his legs for me, he shot forward and wrapped a hand around my shaft. A small gasp left my lips. Not only were his beautiful, long fingers practically dwarfed when wrapped around me like that, but he squeezed me perfectly while stroking up and down a few times.

"I knew you would be," he mumbled, more to himself than to me. "I could tell."

I lowered my lids halfway over my eyes. A deep heat settled into my gut. "Did you?"

Grabbing his wrist, I held him still and rolled my hips back, rearing them forward in a slow motion. He kept his hand firm around me as I fucked myself into his fist, a small and strangled moan leaving him.

"I'm gonna bury myself so damn deep in you, Ayen," I breathed out. I wasn't even pressed against his pretty hole yet and I was already getting lost in the blissful lust. "You want that, don't you?"

He nodded with his lips parted, wet from obsessively licking them. If we had more time, I'd let him take a taste of me. But even now, we were working on borrowed time. Soon, I'd need to radio in to the group and check in so that a search party wasn't sent after us.

While I continued to move my hips, I let go of his wrist in order to drizzle a generous amount of aloe on my fingers, rubbing them together a few times to coat the digits thoroughly.

"Lean back, honey," I said.

Obedient as ever, he let go of my cock and lay back down onto my jacket. He lifted his legs up from the ground automatically, tilting his hips back just enough to reveal himself to me.

I groaned and traced my thumb along his rim, circling around it a few times while his body clenched and unclenched to try and tease one of my fingers inside of him. His balls were drawn up tight, swollen from how much he needed to come.

What a pretty picture he made.

"Fuck, you are gorgeous," I told him, meaning it.

I slipped my thumb inside of him slowly, the heat of his body engulfing me immediately.

"Oh," Ayen mumbled, fanning his legs out more for me.

I pulled out the digit and smeared more aloe over him, coating him generously before working my finger back inside. His head fell back to rest against my jacket.

When I slowly added another finger, he let out a high-pitched whine, his body jolted when I curled them inside to search around for the sweet spot.

"Mmm, right..." He gasped. "There."

I smiled, stroking along the gland a few times until his body was rocking itself to work my fingers deeper as I added a third. He was a damn natural, taking in the intrusion and bearing down just enough to get his body used to it again.

I couldn't wait to sink inside of him, let

him ride me until he came all over the both of us.

"Jax," he murmured.

I slipped my fingers out of his hole, and he clenched around the emptiness a few times with a whine. I grabbed one of his legs and hooked it around me, pulling him closer toward my lap. Slathering more aloe over my cock, I fisted my hand around the head and gave myself a quick few strokes to coat myself.

The head of my cock pressed against his entrance, rubbing along that tight rim until he opened up to me again, begging me to slide in again.

"Ready?"

He nodded wordlessly.

Grabbing onto his other leg, I pushed it down against his chest and held it there while I breached him. He squirmed under me, his nails digging into my arm to hold on while I slowly worked myself into his tight little hole.

Fuck, it was like a damn vice grip, trying to milk me of my cum before I could even get halfway inside of him. I could see how he'd make the perfect little sex doll, being so good for me and letting me do whatever I wanted to him.

Ayen's body jolted again when I rolled my hips, nailing him right in that sweet spot of his that had him choking out a soft 'please' to me.

Jesus, he was going to actually be the death of me.

I started us slow, moving in shallow thrusts until I felt his body open up to me. It didn't take long, his hole greedy and needing to be pounded into like the good little sub he was meant to be.

I kept my hold on his hip firm as I began to pull almost all the way out of him and then slam back inside until my hips were pressed flush against his ass. The soft clapping sounds of our skin making contact with each other was drowned out by the creek next to us, barely heard even as Ayen's body rippled from how hard I was slamming into him.

His moans were loud and so slutty sounding that I had to reach over and grab his chin to force him to look at me as he continued. I needed those sounds directed completely at me. His pupils were blown out, completely lost in the lust of our bodies finally coming together after beating around the bush for so long.

"Fuck," I gritted through my teeth. I wasn't going to last long, not at this rate. He was too much of a turn-on for me to hold back.

Ayen's mouth dropped open while he rapidly pulled in lungfuls of air. I adjusted my hips just enough inside of him to nail his sweet spot with each pass of my cock head.

A few tears leaked from his eyes as he stared at me, so damn gone and lost to the pleasure that was no doubt racking his body.

He painted me the pretty goddamn picture of himself that I was going to burn into my memories for as long as I walked this Earth.

He bared down on me, clenching tight. "J... Jax..."

"Come, baby," I demanded. "You be a good boy and come so that I can fill you up."

His eyes squeezed shut while his body

tensed. Without even having to reach down between us and touch him, his cock began to pump out thick squirts of cum, coating his stomach entirely with it.

I held him down when he began to squirm again, overwhelmed with the pleasure, keeping him pinned while I worked my cock in him as deeply as I could. The caveman part of my brain was taking over, driving me into fucking him hard and fast.

He cried out, his nails digging into my skin again, causing my hips to stutter. My entire body tensed up as I exploded inside of him. Cum poured out of me in what felt like wave after wave, coating him from the inside out as I continued to try and thrust myself inside of him.

Some of my spend leaked out between us, dripping down onto my jacket and causing a sticky mess when I finally slowed and fit my hips against his ass, grinding down to get myself nice and seated.

Ayen collapsed back against the ground, blinking a few times with a dazed look on his face. He was still panting, his skin slicked in a fine layer of sweat that I gave in to my desires and licked a trail up from his stomach to his cheek. He tasted fantastic—just as I thought he would.

A small smile played on his lips, despite his tired and worn out expression.

I kissed along his jaw and up to his mouth, brushing back some sweat-slicked hair from his face.

"Mmm..." He turned to press his cheek against my hand, his words slurred as he said, "That was good..."

Pride swelled in my chest. "Good."

CHAPTER EIGHTEEN

Ayen

HONESTLY, I COULDN'T even remember getting back to my cabin after our trip in the woods.

I think the sex had been so good that it'd melted my brain somehow, completely washing away any other memories outside of Jackson's touch.

How bad was it that I was already craving him again, a few hours after parting for dinner and now alone back in my cabin?

My body was sore, my hole even more so. But it was the good kind of sore; the kind you felt after a really good workout and that the resulting burn afterward felt satisfying instead of punishing.

I wondered how much trouble I'd get into if I snuck out of my cabin tonight and went over to his. With my luck, chances were it'd be a night of random check-ins and I'd get caught trying to sneak back over after Jackson and I had our fill again.

My stupid, addicted brain was already trying to reason with me that it was worth it.

What was a little danger in the face of getting off like that again?

He'd been so gentle afterward. Taking

care to clean me up and kiss me every so often. He'd even dressed me and got me looking somewhat decent before quickly half-assing my kit and walking me back to where the rest of the group, and Roxy, were waiting for us.

She'd come trotting over happily when she'd spotted us, her nose zeroing in on me the second I got within range where she'd sniffed at me for a suspiciously long time.

How embarrassing was it to have a dog sniff out the cum still leaking out of your ass by said dog's owner?

Good thing no one else was paying attention or else Jackson and I would've been screwed.

We'd had to pretend to ignore each other while all of us inmates were dismissed for the evening. And even now, looking back on it, I could feel the heat of his stare following after me as I headed to the mess hall to try and force myself to eat something while my head was still up in the clouds.

And now here I was after lights out, laying alone in my bed and debating with myself on whether or not I should try and chance it.

Whining at my own indecision, I buried my face into my pillow which no longer had the faint scent of Jackson embedded into it. I missed him so fucking much that it was physically hurting me.

I needed him.

Reaching under my covers and back behind me, I snuck a hand under the waistband of my pants and traced my fingers along my sore hole. I couldn't believe he'd been able to fit himself inside of me with that monster cock.

It'd stretched me to the point where I thought I was going to black out, but the pleasure had been too incredible to let go of. He'd known exactly how to work me to get me falling over the edge.

Now I just felt empty, though.

I dipped my fingers into my hole, pretending for a second that they were much thicker and a little more calloused. This wasn't the same, fucking myself with my own fingers, but at least it was better than having nothing at all.

One time being under the man and I was apparently addicted.

Eventually though, my hole grew too sore to continue moving my fingers inside of it, forcing me to slip my hand out of my pants and clench around nothing. Life was unfair. I'd finally gotten to meet a man that I clicked with, both physically and mentally, and yet I couldn't have him.

At least, not in the way that I wanted.

We'd have to resort to sneaking around and hoping like hell we wouldn't get caught.

There was a soft scraping sound coming from over by the cabin door that pulled me out of my wallowing.

Sitting up slightly, I blinked a few times to adjust my eyes to the darkened room.

A figure slipped in through the door, tall and familiar, before closing the door and latching it softly behind him.

My heart leapt into my chest.

"Baby?" came a faint whisper.

My heart clenched at the nickname.

I kicked my sheets off of me and slid over across the bed, making room for him as he slowly shuffled over to me. "Come lay with me."

He let out a soft chuckle and made his way over slowly, patting along the bunks until he found mine and lowered himself slowly down onto the mattress.

I backed my body up into his the moment his arms came around me, pulling me back against his chest while he buried his face into my neck. I felt him breathe in deeply, his body slowly relaxing.

"I missed you," I whispered in the dark.

Jackson squeezed me. "I missed you more. You feeling okay?"

I nodded. "Better than okay."

He chuckled again and kissed a line from my neck up to my jaw. "I love the sound of that."

I traced my fingers along his hand tucked against my chest, feeling the way the tendons flexed under his skin and the pronounced veins that soon disappeared at his forearm. I had half a mind to tell him to pull down my pants but I knew I was still way too sore for that. After going years without sex, my pent up frustrations weren't letting me off that easily.

Jackson moved his hand from my waist to slip under the band of my pants, almost as if reading my mind. He fisted it around my half-hard cock and stroked lazily, breathing out slowly as he buried his face into my neck again.

"I can't get enough of you," he mumbled.

I swallowed, his words, coupled with the sparks of pleasure from his hand moving on me, created a pit of heat that settled low in my gut.

"Jax?"

He hummed softly.

"Do you care? About what I did?"

I hadn't meant for that to be the question that I wanted to ask him—in actuality, I'd wanted to ask him about his life, to get to know him better, but instead, my stupid mouth had let *that one* slip out instead.

His hand didn't pause at all in its movements. His lazy stroking continued as he said, "No."

My gut clenched. "Why not?"

Instead of answering me, he shifted us backward, pulling me along with him as he leaned until he was flat on his back. Tightening his hold around my waist, he scooted me closer, enough until I could comfortably rest the back of my head against his chest. This position gave me room to let my legs fall apart, the motion of his hands tenting my pants more prominent.

I groaned at the feeling of his hand moving on my cock, letting my eyes fall closed.

God*damn,* he know how to work his hand. It was hard to concentrate on anything outside of the rolling pleasure boiling inside of my veins.

"If he wasn't already dead, Ayen, I would've left tonight to go find him," came Jackson's easy response.

My eyes snapped open. "What?"

"You already took care of that though, so."

"No, I didn't."

His hand slowed until it stopped.

"What do you mean?"

I shifted my head to the other side in order to glance up at him. "He's not dead. I was charged with attempted murder in the second degree."

"Second de—? It was self defense?"

I sighed and sat up, grabbing his arm and yanking it out of my pants. So much for just spending the night with him and relaxing. Of course I had to be the dumbass that brought this subject up.

Twisting around, I moved until I was hovering over him, surprised when he pulled me back down to lay on his chest while his arms came to wrap tightly around me again. His hand found its way into my hair, gently moving through the tangled strands.

"Tell me," he said.

"It's a long story."

"I want to hear it anyway."

"No…" I sighed again. "You really don't."

He grew quiet, his hand idly carding through my hair at slow enough pace that it had begun to make me feel drowsy. I blinked a few times, forcing myself to stay awake—*needing to*—while he was still here.

We had such precious little time together. I didn't want to miss any of it because my stupid body was running on fumes.

"My father," Jackson murmured. "He was a lot like your ex-husband. From the sounds of it, anyway."

His tone was even, but being so close to him like this, I could feel the sudden hitch in his voice as he said the words. I hadn't been expecting him to open up to me at all, not like this, anyway. I wanted him to keep talking but I didn't know how to ask.

"We always walked around on eggshells around him," he said after a while. "After my mom died, he changed into a different person. Things got worse."

"I'm sorry." My heart hurt for him. I'd never been close to my parents, but I knew the lost feeling as a child with having no one you could trust in the world. The love of a parent was something that could never be replaced.

"My brother and I were always trying to get him to be proud of us. We were military brats, so you can only imagine the kind of disciplinarian he was."

I winced.

While Alex had never been in the military himself, he'd run our household like the fucking barracks. Back when I was a teenager, if even a single thing was out of place or not to his liking, I got punished. I'd learned his habits quickly, making sure to keep from angering him or else I was sure he'd throw me out onto the streets to fend for myself.

It wasn't much different after we'd gotten married, but at least I had a little say in what went on under that roof. His expectations of me had been astronomical, though, which counteracted most of the privileges I'd been granted once I became his legal spouse.

"Alex was like that," I said softly. "He wasn't military, but…"

Jackson's thumb moved across my cheek. "I'm sorry he treated you that way, Ayen."

"I didn't know any better. He took me

in off the streets when I was sixteen. I was a runaway so I thought he was this... I don't know. Messiah figure. I think that got to his head."

"That seems to be a running theme with abusers." He had a slightly ironic tone that was tinged with sadness. "They get a savior complex after a while."

I sighed. "Yeah. And then blame you for it when reality comes crashing down and they realize they're not shit."

He chuckled softly.

I tilted my head to the side and pressed my ear over his heart. It beat steadily under me, the thrumming sound of it comforting. I raised my hand to grip his bicep.

If anything were to happen to me, I knew Jackson would protect me. He'd done it plenty of times so far and that wasn't even life and death shit.

He was a noble man with a good moral compass. He saw injustice and he fought against it. That was the kind of man that deserved the world.

"At least you had your brother. I'm glad you were there for each other."

Jackson grew quiet again, his fingers pausing in my hair. My body tensed, realizing I'd said something I shouldn't have, though I didn't know what. I waited, with baited breath, for him to speak again.

I needed to stop assuming things like I knew what I was talking about. I was so desperate in wanting to know Jackson that it'd led me to putting my foot in my mouth. Despite us being this close physically, that wasn't my green light to believe I knew anything about him personally.

When he finally spoke, he said, "Used to. He's gone now."

Shit...

"I'm—"

"It's okay," he cut me off. "He was sad for a long, long time."

I squeezed my eyes shut. I could fill in the blanks there to know what had happened. What a damn shame. If he was even half the man that Jackson was, then the world had lost a light when he passed. I ached for Jackson and his loss. It was never fair to lose a loved one far sooner than you expected to.

That was the kind of shit you couldn't prepare for and the blow was always massive.

Thankfully, Jackson began to speak again. "I don't talk to my father anymore.

He doesn't deserve to know what's going on in my life after the bullshit he pulled. I doubt he misses me, anyway. He was always disappointed in me."

That had me shaking my head.

Sitting up, I lifted myself just enough to press my lips against Jackson's. It was hard to see in the dim lighting of the cabin, but I felt him smile, though, and tilted his head to the side, catching my lips fully with his.

"He didn't deserve you," I said when he pulled away, repeating his own words back to him.

"Oh, my sweet, Ayen." He sighed. "Tell me your ex's last name. Was it Gonzalez?"

Oh lord.

"No."

"Tell me."

"Absolutely not."

He brushed the backs of his fingers along my jawline. "Why?"

"Because I'm not letting you go to jail, too."

His smile was practically shit-eating as he said, "What, you don't want to be bunk mates?"

I rolled my eyes and buried my face into his chest before he could see me smiling. I didn't need to be encouraging him into going out and finding my ex-husband and smothering him with a damn pillow while he stared blankly at the ceiling.

Would it be the hottest thing anyone had ever done for me?

Sure, absolutely. But I wasn't going to let this saint-of-a-man wind up behind bars because of me. I wasn't *that* good of a lay.

"Ayen."

I shook my head. "There's no point. He's in a vegetative state."

He huffed out a surprised laugh. "What?"

"That's why I was sentenced. The court felt that I'd purposefully aimed poorly. So, instead of me getting off with self defense, I'd gotten charged with attempted second degree."

"What kind of bullshit is that? Where would they have preferred you to aim?"

"The prosecutor argued that I had plenty of time to hit him in the chest. But I'd aimed for the head instead, resulting in the bullet getting lodged and rendering him pretty much brain dead. The evidence for my defense of him stalking me for four months beforehand was thrown out due to a technicality. So to the jury, it looked like he'd come over to sign the divorce papers and I'd shot him instead."

"*Jesus,*" he choked out.

Weirdly enough, it actually felt good to get all of this off my chest.

In prison, I couldn't exactly talk about what had happened leading up to my crime. Not because I wasn't allowed to or anything, but just because most inmates really didn't give a fuck. There was always someone worse off than you, so trying to gain any kind of sympathy was met with a fist to the face and someone stealing all your commissary.

"Yeah, so." I shrugged. "I got five years."

"You shouldn't have gotten any," he argued.

"Not according to the court."

"I swear to god." Jackson's hand

grabbed at my pant leg and lifted my leg to swing over his hips. He then moved down to grab at my ass, lifting me up until I was practically lying completely on top of him. "Who was your lawyer?"

"A court appointed one."

I could tell he was just barely containing his rage. And while a man getting upset or aggravated around me normally had me wanting to run for the hills, with Jackson it was the complete opposite.

I felt safe. His anger was directed toward those who had hurt me, those he'd protect me against if it came down to it. He let his anger be the fuel that kept me shielded from the danger.

"It's okay," I said, nuzzling my cheek against his chest. "I only have another three years."

"That's three years too long, Ayen. You shouldn't have any at all."

While I agreed, the state had its own opinions. Once I was up in front of a parole board, I'd lament about how sorry I was until they agreed to let me go. I would say just about anything to them if they wanted me to, as long as it got me the fuck out of SAC.

"Have you tried appealing?" His fingers worked their way back through my hair.

"No. My lawyer didn't feel like there was a point with my sentence being less than a decade."

"I'm getting someone to see you. I know a lawyer."

"It's okay, Jax. I'm all right." Well, as good as I could get, I guess. I was on a unit with non-violent offenders, so most of the time, the worst things that were fought about were people being too noisy or inconsiderate while others were trying to sleep.

"I don't want you going back there, Ayen."

Unfortunately, I would have to.

Eventually, this program would end and I would be shipped on a bus back behind the tall, barbed wire walls of SAC until the rest of my three years were finally up.

Did I want that to happen?

Absolutely not, but that was the reality I was facing. Getting worked up about things I couldn't change would only waste precious energy I didn't have.

"I know it sucks."

He let out a slow breath, his chest deflating with the motion.

Guilt began to brew in me, fear that he

was mad at me starting to take root. There was a point in time where I didn't want to care about other people's opinion of me, and had been determined to come here with that same mindset to practice.

How funny that I'd failed so spectacularly at it.

He didn't need to feel sorry for me, or like he had to do something in order to prove to me that he cared. Him simply being here and not treating me like I was a psychopath was enough of a heroic act for me. I didn't need him going out and avenging my honor or something equally as stupid that would land him in serious trouble.

"Jax?"

"Yes, sweetheart."

Ugh, I'd never get enough of the pet names and endearments. They sounded perfect falling from his mouth.

"Stay with me tonight? I usually wake up before the sun comes up. I'll help you leave before headcount starts."

"I'll do you one better." He lifted his hips up off the bed, just enough to retrieve his phone from his pocket. He quickly unlocked it and set an alarm, tossing it onto the bed near the wall. "Now, we can both sleep."

I smiled and relaxed into him, letting my eyes fall closed while the sound of his heart beating under my ear lulled me to sleep.

CHAPTER NINETEEN

Jackson

LEAVING AYEN TO head to my own cabin after spending the night sleeping with him was its own special brand of torture.

I'd woken up before my alarm had gone off, just for the specific purpose of being able to watch him sleep. He was so peaceful with his head lying on my chest and the gentle noises of him breathing deeply cutting into the silence inside of the cabin.

I'd gotten hardly any sleep myself at all last night. Instead, I spent most of the night lying awake thinking about Ayen's ex, his disaster of a trial, the way he'd been treated before he'd ever been arrested, all of it. I couldn't stand the injustice that my baby bird had faced in his only two decades on this god-forsaken planet.

Where had the people who were supposed to be fighting for him gone?

His parents were out of the picture, but what about his ex's parents?

Where the fuck were they in all of it?

Every new piece of information that he told me had solidified my hatred for the man who'd done this—who'd started it all. Ayen had pulled the trigger, but that man had been the one to place the gun in his hand, even if he hadn't done so physically.

And the fact that the courts completely dismissed that was beyond me.

By the time I got back to my cabin, Roxy was already up and whining for food. After quickly feeding her, I popped into the shower to wash away the residual anger that I still felt. I wasn't even sure if that would ever go away—not when at the end of this program, I'd be forced to let Ayen go back to the one place he absolutely did not belong.

How he'd managed this far to still stay so soft and sweet was beyond me, but I'd be damned if I wasn't going to protect him in the future from further misery.

Once clean and dressed again, I grabbed my phone and scrolled through my contacts, hitting the 'call' option once

I reached the one I'd been looking for. I pressed the receiver to my ear while I headed back into the kitchen, my body restless and needing something to do.

"'lo?" A groggy voice on the other end answered me.

"Nina? It's Jax."

She groaned loud enough to be insulting. "What the fuck, why are you calling me at... six-fucking-thirty. Are you serious, Jackson?"

"I need a favor."

"Fuck you," she grumbled.

"It's serious, Nina. I wouldn't be calling you like this out of the blue if it wasn't."

There was a long sigh on the other end, followed by some rustling around as she most likely was sitting herself up and getting out of bed. While I waited, I grabbed the box of instant pancake mix and set it down on the counter.

Roxy trotted over to me, curiously poking her nose at my thigh while I grabbed a mixing bowl from the cupboard.

"Okay," Nina finally said, sounding much more alert. "What is it?"

"Can I meet with you? It's probably better if we talk in person."

"Geezus, Jax. You wake me up at six in the fucking morning... to ask me to meet with you later? This couldn't have been a text because...?"

Despite her surly attitude, I knew Nina would go to the ends of the Earth to help me. It was just in her nature, too. She was a bleeding heart like me; the constant desire to help the unhelpable was like a sickness that could only be cured through situations like this.

I'd known Nina for close to my entire life and not once had I ever seen her *not* rip the shirt off her own back to give it to someone else that needed it more.

"I had to make sure you actually looked at it instead of ignoring it like the other ten messages I've sent you."

There was a pause on the other end before she mumbled, "Touché."

Pouring some mix into the bowl, I measured out the wet ingredients with one hand before tossing my measuring cup into the sink next to me. "It's about an inmate in my rehabbing program. I want to help him and I think you can help me with that."

"Oh, Jackson." She sighed. "If they're already sentenced, there's not much I can do."

"I think his can easily be overturned if

we got the paperwork to the right judge."

At least, that was what I was hoping for. I had no fucking clue how the justice system worked outside of what a normal person walking down the street knew. I'd worked with inmates for a long time, sure, but them talking about their charges or what went into them receiving them in the first place was never discussed.

Me getting privy info from the COs had been a miracle and one that I knew would never happen again.

Everything that I learned after this was either going to be through Ayen, or hopefully, Nina.

"You say that like I have a magic wand. I'm not superwoman, you know that, right?"

"Yeah, but you're also the best damn lawyer that I know," I argued, setting my skillet down onto my stove and turning up the heat.

"I'm the *only* damn lawyer you know."

"I have other friends!"

"Name two. And don't say Mac, you fucking loser."

I rolled my eyes practically to the back of my head. "What's wrong with being friends with my coworkers?"

"Well, for one, what else do you guys talk about besides work?"

"Look, not everyone can dish like we do."

"We're gay, Jackson. No one can."

I huffed out a laugh. "All right, fine. Whatever. Can you please meet me in town later today? He's only got five more weeks here, so I need you to look at his case file, pronto."

"I'll look at it but I can't promise you

anything."

"That's fine. I just need another set of eyes on it because it's driving me insane."

"Why?" she asked.

"You'll see." Roxy whined at me again, her big doe eyes reminding me instantly of the man I'd had to leave behind an hour prior. "Text me when you want to meet. I'll take the day off today and meet you whenever."

"Fine. But you're paying for our food."

"Deal."

When the other end of the line dropped, I pulled my phone away from my ear and set it down onto the counter next to me. While I believed in Nina and her skills as a defense lawyer, she had a point. She wasn't a miracle worker and simply thinking that Ayen's case could easily be overturned given the right circumstances didn't mean that those would ever be presented in the first place.

The justice system was already fucked as it was for innocent people. It was downright rigged if you were ever convicted of anything, even if it was false or not. The odds were stacked against you the moment a pair of cuffs was slapped onto your wrists.

Though even with all of that, I still couldn't let Ayen go back without a fight. It'd eat me alive if I did. If there was even a shred of a chance in getting him out of prison and giving him the freedom he so truly deserved, then I'd do whatever I could to see it through.

Even if by the end of it all he chose to stop seeing me.

All I cared about was getting him out of a place where he never should've been.

Anyone with half a brain would think the same if they knew the facts. And I was sure once I got a hold of his case file, and saw the dark and horrible truth, that feeling inside of me would only grow.

There was no doubt in my mind that he was wrongfully convicted.

Probation for ten years, sure.

But prison?

No. It was too far for my baby bird.

Roxy whined again, pulling me out of my thoughts.

I reached over and placed a hand on her head, rubbing along her temple toward the back of her skull.

"I know, girl. I miss him, too. But we'll see him soon."

Her big brown eyes didn't look all too convinced.

Actually... since I was going to be

taking the day off from here in order to meet up with Nina, I'd need someone to watch Roxy in the meantime.

Who better than the inmate she was whining to see?

"You want to go see Ayen?" I asked her.

Her tail began to wag.

At least while I was gone she could keep him company.

Not to mention it would give me an excuse when coming back here to meet up with him again without the COs catching wind of what was going on between us.

It was the perfect plan.

Roxy let out a soft 'woof' in what I imagined as stark approval.

"All right, girl. Give me a second and then we'll go see him."

CHAPTER TWENTY

Jackson

"THANKS FOR MEETING me."

Nina lowered herself into the seat across from me, her wide-rimmed sunglasses still perched on her nose. The bag she'd brought with her, a large leather satchel that I recognized from her court hearings, was set down onto the chair next to her.

"Did I have a choice?" she asked,

though there was no real bite behind her words.

"Funny."

Her sharply cut hair, angled down toward her chin, was slicked back with the arms of her sunglasses as she slid them onto the top of her head. Her beautifully done eye makeup had a dark and smoky look to it, bringing out the clear blues of her eyes, and was angled in a way that complimented her angular features.

Under the table, I was bouncing my leg like crazy. My pent up nerves from coming back from the courthouse early this morning with the thick folder sitting next to me on the table felt like it was burning a hole in me. I'd chanced a look through it while I'd been waiting for her, only getting to the fifth page before a sick twisting in my gut had forced me to stop.

There weren't any evidence pictures attached to the documents, but the descriptions alone had made me nauseous. How Ayen went through any of that and still got convicted was beyond me when there were so many more violent offenders out there still walking the streets.

I'd managed to cash in a favor at the county court's office from an officer friend of mine—who had not so subtly given me a sideways look when I'd told him what I needed to get passed along to me—but had, thankfully, been able to pull some strings and get me the papers without much fuss from the county clerk.

Now, I didn't know what to do with them. How we would get any of this in front of a judge was beyond me, but that's where Nina came in.

Hopefully.

"So," Nina's voice brought me out of my thoughts. "What's made you about this inmate so much? Aside from your ridiculously sensitive moral compass."

I slid the file over to her. "Just take a look—"

Her hand slapped down on top of it, preventing me from moving it any further. "Jax, be honest with me."

Tension burned inside me.

My and Nina's relationship dated way back, far enough that we'd both consider each other childhood friends even if we didn't exactly meet as 'kids'. She was essentially a part of my life, despite us hardly seeing each other these days.

With her firm taking off the moment she'd made partner, and me running the work program for inmates, we were lucky if we got to texting each other for more than an hour or two every few weeks.

Still, regardless of all of that, I knew I could trust her. At least with helping me figure out if Ayen had a real shot in getting this entire case thrown out or not.

Her knowing about me being intimately involved with him, though?

That was the more dicey question.

"I feel bad for him." Not exactly the entire truth, but true nonetheless.

She raised a brow. "That's it?"

"What more do you want from me?"

"I just didn't think you were spending enough time with any of them that would get you close enough to get their side of the story."

"When you work with people long enough, you start to see their humanity,"

I said.

Her sigh was long, but she didn't argue with me. Lifting her hand away from the file, she let me slide it closer to her, flipping open the front flap to look over the cover page detailing the highlights of Ayen's case.

While she read silently, I ordered us a light lunch and two coffees, needing the caffeine myself from barely sleeping last night. No matter what I did, I replayed Ayen's words in my head so many times that I had them memorized by now.

The hitch in his voice when he spoke, the dead tone of him telling me it was pointless to even try to get his sentence overturned, all of it. And while he lay sleeping peacefully on my chest, I'd promised myself that I wouldn't let this go no matter how hard he fought me on it.

That son-of-a-bitch husband wasn't going to win and taint Ayen's life for the rest of eternity. I wouldn't let him.

Halfway through finishing my plate of food, Nina finally pulled her head out of the documents. "Jesus, this kid has had it rough."

I nodded and chewed slowly.

If she saw half of what I did just from that file alone, I knew Ayen had a real chance. Nina was a viper in the courtroom. A lawyer not to go toe-to-toe with if you knew what was good for you. She'd gotten that reputation from college and had allowed it to be carried with her all the way to the firm she worked at now, not letting the 'boy's club' stop her from doing some great things for people.

I admired her every damn day for not giving up and making something of herself that my late brother would be proud of.

She sighed. "I'll be honest, this is going to be a tough one."

Lowering my fork, I said, "You don't think he can be proven innocent?"

"It's not that. The problem is that a lot of his evidence proving spousal abuse wasn't put in front of a jury. So all it seems like from that perspective is spousal estrangement gone wrong."

"We can't get all of that in front of another jury?"

She shook her head. "He wouldn't be going for a re-trial since he was already convicted. I could see about getting a judge to look at it, but you know those asswipes. They protect each other and if one degenerate decided on something, there's not typically any other judge who will actually go against the original judgment. Especially, if they're in the same county circuit."

Leaning back in my seat, I let myself sit with the information.

Ayen's original lawyer had told him that going up in front of a judge for a dismissal was pointless, and while at the time I'd thought that was complete bullshit—and still do—maybe it was because of the abhorrent politics within the justice system.

Forcing my baby bird to relive any of that shit in order to have the slim chance of a possible overturned conviction was a big ask, and understandably, not something he should be put through again.

But on the other end of the tossed coin, what *if* it was the thing that got him out of prison?

What *if* putting this file in front of a judge—the right one this time—got him set free and his record wiped in exchange for parole and time served?

I doubted he'd even care about the parole part, anyway.

"I need him out of there, Nina." My voice was soft as I spoke.

Her eyes widened briefly, caught off guard by my sudden confession. It wasn't every day that I opened up and bared my soul like this, especially about a taboo subject involving an inmate that I absolutely had no business getting entangled with.

This was the real deal, though. My feelings for Ayen were all encompassing, to the point where the four weeks I had left with him were feeling like hours now.

Our time together was slowly dwindling away by the ticking of a grandfather clock, ominously waiting to chime at midnight.

I couldn't let him slip through my fingers and be lost to the system for another three years.

What happened if someone were to hurt him while he was there?

There was no guarantee that he'd be safe, regardless of what part of the prison he was in. Anyone at any time could deem him as a threat and take him out.

I could never forgive myself if that happened. Not when I could do something to try and prevent it altogether.

Whatever Nina saw in my eyes had her slowly nodding her head at me, a thoughtful look crossing over her face while she placed her hand over the stack of papers.

"If you're actually serious about this, if *he* is, then I need to talk to him," she said.

"I can set that up."

She nodded again. "Let me know when. I'm going to take this with me and head back to the firm. I'm going to have some of my colleagues look it over. If there's a possibility that we can get this overturned for wrongful conviction, then we're going to need all the damn help we can get."

I breathed out a slow breath, relief washing over me. "Thank you, Nina."

"Don't thank me just yet. Get your boy on board and then we'll talk."

Warmth curled in my belly.

My boy.

I loved the sound of that.

CHAPTER TWENTY-ONE

Jackson

AFTER PARTING WAYS with Nina, I climbed back into my truck and hit the road.

Being that it was only a little past one, the inmates and my coworkers would still be out on the trails training, it gave me very little to do back at the property without even my dog to keep me company.

I supposed I could pass the time going to the gym or even heading back to my cabin to get it cleaned and ready to sneak Ayen over later tonight. Hell, there was also probably a mound of paperwork that needed to be tackled back at the property office for the next batch of recruits coming in less than four weeks.

Plenty to do while I waited for the sun to set and the program to get back from their day adventure.

Something burned in my mind, though.

An address to a care facility only a few miles away from here.

Drumming my fingers along the steering wheel, I glanced back in my rearview to the traffic idling behind me. All I had to do was turn at this next light and I'd be on my way to CWI Generations.

I could see for myself the one man who had gotten my baby bird thrown in prison.

The light shifted up ahead, the two cars in front of me slowly letting off the brakes and moving forward. I ghosted my finger over my turn signal, indecision freezing me.

Ayen didn't want me to get involved, explicitly told me not to, in fact.

I wanted to behave, especially for him. Even though it was killing me not to know. Not to face his ex and look him in his dead eyes and curse him for what he'd done.

Behind me, a horn blared.

Fuck it.

I pushed down onto the turn signal.

CHAPTER TWENTY-TWO

Ayen

"DOES ANYONE HAVE any questions before we wrap up for the night?" The firefighter's voice boomed over the group. When no one answered, he waved his hand. "Return your gear and head to the mess hall. Good work today, gentlemen."

Shrugging off my heavy coat and letting it drop onto the ground behind me felt amazing, especially when a soft breeze trickled in through the trees and washed over my sweaty body.

Roxy let out a bark when I bent to pick up the coat again, her tail wagging happily. I brushed my hand over her head a few times, smoothing back her soft coat.

"Did you have fun today as my partner?" I smiled when she barked at me again. "Yeah, me too."

Talking to a dog like she was human no doubt had me looking a little insane. But with no partner to keep me company all day, I found myself replacing my human interaction with Jackson's dog instead. To no surprise, she was incredibly well trained and took commands like a champ.

He'd given me a crash course of it this morning before jetting off into the city for whatever reason. All day, my thoughts had been tripping up on him, wondering what in the world he'd skip out on training for when he was the one who was supposed to be running the program.

Of course, my mind had immediately gone into full disaster-mode and convinced myself for half of the fucking day that he was out meeting with someone else.

Could I even call that cheating when we weren't exactly in a stable relationship?

It sure felt like a fucking stab to the chest every time my mind got itself worked up. Thankfully, Roxy was my rock and had worked me down from going actually insane to only slightly fucked up.

After handing in my gear, I led Roxy through the property, following after the other inmates heading to the mess hall.

While passing by, I took a glance over to the staff parking lot; Jackson's truck was still missing from the lot.

It was hard to not let that bother me. I missed him horribly, more than I wanted to admit to myself. The longer I dwelled on his absence, the more it was making it all the more difficult in ignoring my very obviously budding feelings.

"Hey, Gonzalez," someone called out to me. Turning, I spotted one of the firefighters, Mac. "I'm going to walk the dog back to the staff cabins. Thanks for looking after her today."

My heart squeezed. "Oh. Uh, sure."

Roxy's doe-eyes turned to me, a whine leaving her when Mac tapped on her collar and whistled at her to follow after him. I stayed rooted to my spot while they walked away. If I knew I was going to be giving her back so soon before seeing Jackson, I would've at least savored the remaining time we had together.

Now I really was all alone.

I dragged my feet as I headed into the mess hall. The food tasted like ash while I ate, tucked away in the back away from everyone.

While in prison, I'd gotten used to being alone. I'd spent most of my formative years surrounded by someone all-encompassing, his presence bleeding into every aspect of my life until I reached a point of not even being able to breathe without him there.

Prison had given me a harsh reality check into my co-dependence issues. Slapping me in the face with how much of my life I had relied on someone loving me. The past two years, I'd kept everyone at a distance, even Tyson. We were friends, of course, but the kind that you left at work when you went home for the day.

Jackson had been my first taste of the forbidden fruit after having gone sober for so long. He'd sunk down deep into my bones and made a home there, rooted indefinitely.

How could I start to pluck the blossoms that grew from it so soon after they'd begun to bloom?

I couldn't be that cruel to myself, even with my subconscious screaming at me to stop before he got hurt. My lingering need for him was an unrelenting beast that I'd need to put down eventually. For the sake of both of us.

Regardless of how much it killed me to think about.

By the time I finished up and made my

way to the communal showers, I was starting to feel the fatigue from the day settle over me. We hadn't done a lot of hiking today but the gear we'd put on had been heavy and hot under the sun.

Learning how to move in gear like that gave me an even more impressive outlook on Jackson's job. Without adding the actual firefighter or search and rescue parts to the mix, the guy had a lot of guts getting into situations like that. It took a special breed of person to brave a natural disaster and keep a level head.

The hot water sluicing over my skin melted all of my stress away, leaving me feeling boneless and ready for an early bedtime. I disregarded the other inmates tossing their towels around and snapping them against each other's asses while getting dressed, and quickly hustled out before I became an unwilling participant.

Getting back to my cabin, I was surprised to see the inside door slightly ajar but didn't think much of it, until I stepped inside and caught sight of the figure sitting on my bed.

"Woah, woah," Jackson said, quickly getting up and putting his hands out toward me when I jumped hard enough to knock into the front door. "It's okay. It's just me."

I slapped a hand to my chest, exhaling shakily. "What... the hell..."

He chuckled, though his eyes were sympathetic. "I'm sorry. I didn't mean to scare you. You okay?"

Lifting myself away from the door, I peeked out the window to where the dying sun was still coloring the horizon.

Why was Jackson here so early?

Wasn't he afraid of getting caught when it was still light out?

"Ayen?"

My head snapped over to look at him. "Oh, sorry."

He gestured for me to come closer to him, holding out his arms to me. I practically leaped into them, letting him sweep me up off of my feet and cradle me to his chest while he settled back down on my bunk. I instinctually buried my face into the crook of his neck, pulling in a lungful of his musky scent.

Fuck, I missed him.

As sad as it was to actually feel my entire body begin to relax, I was grateful that he hadn't waited until late tonight to come see me.

He brushed his hand along the back of my hair, threading his fingers through the wet lengths while he placed soft kisses against my temple. "You do okay today? Roxy treat you well?"

I nodded, letting my eyes drift closed. Honestly, I could fall asleep right here and not even care.

"Good," he said.

"You?" I mumbled.

"My day was okay. For the most part."

Pulling away from him, my brows knit together and I stared at his face, taking in the tired expression. "What were you up to today?"

His arms were still locked tightly around me, only shifting slightly down toward my hips when he ducked under the lip of the bunk above us and pulled me with him as he leaned back against the wall. We were kind of crunched in under there but it felt safe like that. Like we were in our own little pillow fort.

"I met with a friend today," he said, his hands squeezing my hips. "A lawyer friend."

My stomach dropped. "Jax..."

"I told her about your case. She's interested in it."

I sighed. "Well, she's going to get real uninterested pretty soon. There's nothing that can be done when I only have a few more years left."

Jackson brushed his hand along my jaw, a slight frown tugging down on his lips. "I know you think that, but three years is still a long time. Especially, when you shouldn't be serving any time at all."

I shrugged. I'd come to terms with my situation long ago. Wasting time lamenting about it would do nothing for either of us. "I get that, but that's how it works in the States. You get fucked and then you have to deal with it."

Jackson shook his head. "No. Not this time. We're going to do something about it."

"I appreciate your confidence, but—"

"Baby, I looked through your file. You have a very strong case."

I froze in place.

My file?

He saw...

His hands tightened around me when I tried to lift myself off of him. "I'm not scared of it, Ayen. You did what you had to do. Reading over your case only solidified my opinion of that fact."

My eyes began to burn.

He was never supposed to see that.

My shame, my guilt.

The horrible things I'd had to talk

about in court, only for them to get thrown out in the end for bullshit reasons that I still couldn't grapple with.

Jackson was supposed to remain ignorant to all of that. I'd given him the cliff notes version, the important highlights that were heavily filtered so that I could spare him the fucking gory details about what went on between Alex and I and the fallout afterward.

I knew, eventually, that my public record would be the fucking death of me, but I thought that would come three years from now when I was applying for a job as a busser at a seedy restaurant.

"Hey..." He cupped my face. "None of that."

His lips were soft against my cheek, kissing my tear away as it slipped from my eye.

"Why did you look," I choked out.

"Because I wanted to understand you and prove to you that what I said was real. I haven't changed my mind at all about you, baby."

"But—"

He made a negative sound in his throat, tightening the arm around my waist in order to crush me against his chest. He was gentle as he ran his fingers through my hair again, not at all caring when my tears made the front of his shirt wet.

"My friend said that she's bringing your case to her partners at the firm she works at. She's a fucking shark, so I know what she's going to do everything possible to get your case at least put in front of a new judge." His voice was soft as he spoke. "I'm getting you out of there, Ayen.

I swear I will."

"What if you can't?" I had to force the words out of my mouth. "What... if nothing changes?"

He was quiet for a long time but his heartbeat remained steady under my ear.

"Then I'll wait."

So simple.

Just like that.

Like it was an easy decision to make.

Maybe it was.

Maybe this was what I was... what *we* were meant to be doing. For some reason, maybe a sign from the damn universe itself, this program had come to me at a time when I needed it most. I'd been brought here to meet this man who was now promising me a future, something that I never thought I'd have again.

He was showing me that there was

more to life than letting my past ruin me.

I lifted my head and leaned forward to kiss him. "Stay with me tonight?"

He smiled against my lips. "I'd love to."

CHAPTER TWENTY-THREE

Jackson

I SLEPT WELL with Ayen cradled against me, his warm body acting like my own personal space heater and keeping me toasty all night long while our bodies were entangled with each other.

He fit perfectly, practically molded against my body like a second skin that was always meant to be there. I loved it. I loved everything about the situation and only regretted having to wake us both up once the sun was beginning to lighten the sky outside of the cabin's window.

I brushed my lips along the column of his neck, sucking just hard enough to wake him but not enough to leave marks behind like I was dying to. When I got him out of this mess, and I could finally take him home back to my place in the city, I'd make sure that every inch of his perfect tan skin was flushed red from my teeth.

I rolled my hips against his, both of us already half hard.

A soft moan escaped him, breathy and still half asleep. He craned his neck back, giving me more access to run my tongue up to the shell of his ear.

I wanted to take my time with him, savor all of this. He was meant to be taken slowly, lovingly, with the time and care and dedication of a seasoned lover who knew how to worship him the way I'd been dying to since I first laid eyes on him.

He moaned again when I moved my hand under his shirt, caressing his stomach and the faint happy trail leading down to the waistband of his pants. He ground his hips up against mine, teasing me with his eagerness.

I rolled him over onto his back and moved on top of him, pining him down against the mattress with my hips against his. His lashes fluttered open, showing me those pretty doe-eyes of his that were still hazy from sleep.

God, he was so fucking gorgeous it was honestly unfair.

Bending down, I caught his lips with mine, loving how easily he parted them for me to slip my tongue between. I dipped my hand under his waistband while I shifted my hips up just enough to wrap my hand around his pretty little cock.

It stiffened instantly with a few long pumps, drawing another groan out of him.

That sound was music to my damn ears.

He brushed his hands over my pecs with his gentle touches all the way down to where my jeans were belted. He rubbed me over top of the material, making my cock jerk against my leg where it was pinned inside of my pants.

I pulled away from our kiss, nipping him until I reached his ear again. "Tease."

He chuckled softly.

Letting go of his cock, I pulled my

hand out from his pants and moved it around to the small of his back, getting ready to lift him up and pull him into my lap.

Before I could though, Ayen's shifted his hand from where he had been rubbing me through my jeans and slipped it into my pocket in order to tease me some more. I groaned when he brushed the fabric of my pocket against the sensitive tip of my cock while retrieving something from it.

I was barely paying attention to anything other than getting him flustered and naked under me and it wasn't until his body stiffened under me that I was broken out of my own haze.

Ayen shoved an elbow at my chest, practically knocking me right off of the bed from the force of it. At the last second, I grabbed onto the lip of the top bunk to catch myself. "Baby—"

"W-What the *hell is this*?"

As soon as I turned to look at him again, my entire body froze. Pinched between his fingers was the folded over sticker of the visitor pass I'd been given yesterday by CWI.

His hand was shaking, eyes wide in disbelief as he stared at it.

Fuuuck!

"Ayen, listen. I can explain." A stabbing pain shot through my chest when he skittered away from my outstretched hand, lunging off of the bed in order to press himself against the wall farthest away from me.

"Why do you have this?"

"Baby..." I lifted off of the bunk.

"Why do you have this!" His eyes were

filling with tears again, although this time it wasn't out of pleasure.

I wasn't sure what to say.

How could I explain any of that to him?

My heart knocked against my ribcage. "Ayen..."

He took in two shuddering breaths before he said, "Did you visit him?"

I nodded. There was no point in lying when he was holding the evidence right in his hand. I didn't want to, anyway, although I would've rather he found out about this much differently.

Going to visit his ex-husband had been eye opening, more so than I could've ever imagined before stepping into that situation.

Ayen was shaking his head, mumbling 'no' over and over again.

"It's okay." My voice was soft as I spoke. "Nothing's changed."

"Did you see him?"

I hesitated before nodding again, imploring him with my gaze, begging him to try to understand.

He let out a pitiful sob and slowly slid down the wall until he collapsed onto the ground. My instincts were screaming to go to him, to pull him up into my arms and rock him until his grief passed.

What I saw in that care facility had been shocking, but not because it had been caused at the hands of Ayen. True disgust had filled me when I saw the man who had abused my baby bird for so long was being well taken care of by the staff there with, presumably, his parents' money lining their pockets.

The anger I felt, the unadulterated

rage, was a feeling I'd only ever felt one other time in my life before, and that had been at Carter's funeral where I'd witnessed my dad shedding a single tear over his casket while it was being lowered into the dirt.

Ayen's ex didn't deserve to have a healthy amount of weight on him, or to be clean and smelling fresh when I'd approached him in his wheelchair, or the privilege of being able to stare out the window where a bird feeder was hanging to entertain what little was left of his mind.

What that scum of the earth had earned was a one-way ticket to hell, and nothing less.

Instead, he got to spend the rest of his life being taken care of like a baby while my *own* was stuck behind bars.

Not wanting to scare him, I lowered myself down onto the floor as close as I could get. "Honey..."

His legs were drawn up to his chest, arms curled tightly around his knees, while his shoulders shook from his sobs. It was brutal to watch, and even worse to think that he believed I saw him any differently than before because of it.

I would never. I *could* never.

"Go..." he finally choked out.

I shook my head, reaching over to breech the distance between us. "Ayen—"

He slapped my hand away the second it touched him. "Go!"

Stunned, I stared at him.

"Leave," he swallowed. "Or I'll scream."

That aching sharp pain stabbed me in the chest again. Robotically, I climbed to my feet, still staring down at him. Hoping that he'd change his mind. But all he did was simply bury his face back into his knees and hold himself tighter.

The air in my lungs was sucked out breath by breath as I crossed the distance between him and the front door.

Regret was a knife that carved my heart out of my chest when I opened the door and snuck out into the morning sun, leaving it behind.

CHAPTER TWENTY-FOUR

Ayen

I HAD NO idea how long I stayed curled up on the floor for.

Minutes?

Hours?

It was hard to tell. I'd eventually exhausted myself to the point of lying down on the dusty and worn hardwood floor, with my cheek pressed against it. My body had shut down the second I closed my eyes, wanting to forget any of this ever happened.

A loud call was what brought me back, the sound of Barlow roll calling everyone.

I contemplated staying there curled up in a ball and getting written up for it.

How bad would my punishment be compared to the deep betrayal I felt?

In the grand scheme of things, everything else simply paled in comparison.

Eventually, though, I forced myself up and wandered outside to the line-up, barely functioning.

"Gonzalez, why the fuck're you still in your pjs?" Stinner said.

My gaze drifted up to where he loomed over me, his shadow temporarily blocking out the sun burning my eyes. No words came out of my mouth—not even a single thought. My mind was blank, my body running on simply muscle memory alone.

"Get the fuck back inside and get dressed. Jesus Christ," he spat.

Turning back around, I headed into my cabin again without any kind of arguing. Getting myself together was a blur, as was the rest of our head count and heading into the mess hall for breakfast before we got started for the day.

That sticker was branded into my skin—Jackson's handsome face grainy and barely decipherable on the horrible laser scanner that had been used to print up a visitor pass for him.

The worst part was that if I'd never found it, he never would've told me.

How long would he have gone carrying on the ignorance?

For the rest of our weeks together?

After that, too?

I'd told him—*begged him*—not to go find Alex. But he'd done so, anyway.

To what, prove to himself that it 'wasn't that bad'?

That I wasn't the type of person who was capable of such a violent act?

Whatever he'd told himself in order to convince himself that he was fine with seeing Alex like that was a complete lie. *No one* could handle something like that; no matter how prepared you were going into it.

A bright and charismatic man being reduced down to someone who pissed and shit in a diaper all day wasn't the kind of thing you simply witnessed and got over while convincing yourself that he deserved it.

The reality was that, eventually, Jackson was going to come to his senses and see just what kind of monster I was to leave someone in that state, regardless on whether or not it was accidental. Soon, he'd see the real reason I was meant to be behind bars and our little fantasy together would come crashing down.

I was sick to my stomach when he'd asked the first time for Alex's info, knowing that by walking down that road I was essentially letting what we had slip right through my fingers. That's why I'd begged him to let it go, to just forget it.

But of course, Jackson being Jackson could never do that. He had to see the disgusting mess for himself and try to prove that he wasn't like everyone else who saw me for the murderer I was.

"All right, everyone!" Mac's voice

snapped me back into reality. "Partner up!"

Blinking a few times to clear my head, I realized that I'd somehow transported myself from the mess hall to a designated training area where there were work stations set out for us to gather around.

Across the way, I caught eyes with Jackson who was watching me with a pinched expression on his face. Roxy stood at his side, wagging her tail while she pranced in place from where Jackson was holding onto her work vest.

Immediately turning away from them, I gathered around the closest workstation where another inmate, James Barker, was already standing.

He glanced over at me when I stood next to him, his arms crossing over his chest.

"You're my partner for this," I forced myself to say.

He gave me a weird look before shrugging. "Whatever."

CHAPTER TWENTY-FIVE

Ayen

FOR THE NEXT week, everything went the same way—me avoiding Jackson like the plague and him keeping his distance from me.

There were no more midnight rendezvous, no more quiet meetings when no one else was looking, no more subtle brushes of our hands together as we walked back from the training area and parted ways at the mess hall.

I felt the void of him in everything that I did. From sunrise to sunset, my body hurt from how hard I was punishing it in order to keep my feelings tamped down far enough to numb me from the inside.

I kept a rotation of partners during our training, keeping myself preoccupied and not giving it up to fate or chance that I'd be randomly placed with Jackson and Roxy.

Nothing felt right.

My soul ached.

And there was fuck all I could do about it.

"Can you get your fucking head on straight, Gonzalez?" Barker hissed while tossing a large pack at me.

I stumbled back, catching it in the chest.

"You know, when you said you wanted to be my partner, I didn't know you were going to be fucking useless."

The words barely stung. He was all bark, anyway.

Quietly, I set the pack down and looked through the contents, ignoring Barker's huffing as he repacked his own the way he wanted it. Judging by the contents, we were most likely heading out to the fire that was burning a few miles east from here.

The call had come in late last night, all of the firefighter's radios blaring with the emergency signal. So far, the fire hadn't spread rapidly, but it was burning enough to keep the property's firefighters set up as reinforcements.

Mac had suggested for us to head over there this morning and using it as a learning opportunity for a once-in-a-lifetime deal at seeing how a real forest fire was dealt with. The excitement had been palpable among the rest of the inmates, excluding me, who were more than ready to actually put some of this training into action.

Now that we were all here and successfully piled off of the bus that'd brought us, Mac was explaining something that I tuned out completely. Even with us being a mile out from the fire, the air was hazy with smoke and the smell of burning wood.

"You coming or what, Gonzalez?" Barker said, throwing his pack over his shoulder. His fire-resistant coveralls bunched up at his shoulders, making it difficult for him to straighten out the straps of his bag.

"Make sure you keep within the radius of the firefighters," Mac called out. "If any of you stray off the path, use your whistle to call out and one of us will come find you. If you start to feel intense heat or thick smoke, fall back immediately and use your whistle!"

I sighed and zipped my bag up before tossing it over my shoulder and working my arms through the straps. It was heavy on my back but not to the point where it would slow me down. Luckily, we were only going to be getting close enough to observe from a distance and take some pictures that we would later observe back at the property.

There would be no heroics going on today, thankfully.

Just as I was about to follow Barker over to where our group was gathering, something grabbed my bag from behind me and made me halt in place. Without me even getting a chance to look behind me, something tugged at one of the loops at my waist, hooking something on it.

I darted my gaze down, spotting a familiar radio now clipped there.

My heart stuttered when I looked up again just as Jackson was moving around me and heading back toward the rest of the group, Roxy following closely behind.

What?

Ghosting my fingers over the radio and ignoring the way my chest suddenly tightened, I quickly followed after Barker who had our camera looped around his neck. In a wide formation, we started in through the tree lines at a slow pace.

I wasn't sure what the hell we were supposed to be taking pictures of, having completely checked out by the time we'd climbed onto the bus, but now I was regretting not paying attention. Especially, when Barker started to hiss at me once more.

"Can you keep up? I want to get good photos."

"Why?"

Honestly, what was the point?

It wasn't like we were receiving extra credit for any of this.

"Does it fucking matter?" he snapped back and kicked his way through a tall bush.

We were moving a bit of a distance away from the rest of the group, though I could still see them through the haze. The reflectors on their jackets helped with their visibility to me, becoming even more pronounced when I pulled my goggles down over my eyes to keep them from watering.

"I was just wondering," I said.

"Well, if you have to know, I want to get as close a picture as possible. I overheard Browne talking about bringing some of our accomplishments to the Warden and getting us special privileges when we get back. We're apparently the best group they've had so far."

Somehow, I doubted that, but hey, if living in a little fantasy world kept Barker happy, then who was I to spoil it?

All I wanted to do was keep my mind off the very obvious thing plaguing it.

I brushed my hand over the radio again in disbelief.

Why had he gone out of his way to give it to me?

Setting me up to be caught with it was

a possibility, but even Jackson couldn't be that cruel. There would be no reason for him to do that when we were already actively avoiding each other.

He hadn't even looked at me, either. Just gave it to me and dipped.

I hated how much that man haunted me.

"Woah, Gonzalez, look!"

Breaking out of my thoughts, I stumbled and ran right into Barker's back, causing us both to fall into the dirt.

"Jesus, fuck! Watch it," he spat out.

I grunted and slowly pushed myself up onto my hands and knees, watching him do the same out of the corner of my eye. The haze had grown thicker in the time we'd spent walking this way. Even through my coveralls, I could feel the telltale signs of heat.

I grabbed at the scarf hanging around my neck and pulled it up over my nose.

"What I was trying to fucking say before you fucking shoved me," Barker went on, getting to his feet again. "Was that I think I see fire."

"Fire?" I lifted my head. "We should head back then."

"No way. Shots this close up are gold. I'm not passing that up."

Getting to my feet, I brushed the dirt off of myself. "We're not getting caught up in a damn forest fire, you idiot."

"We'll be fine." He waved his hand. "We're too high up for it to get us."

"What?"

What the hell did that even mean?

"Did you not pay attention to any of the demonstrations? The air is thick up here because of the smoke rising. That means the fire is down farther. I bet there's a hill we can stand on to see it."

"We're not getting that close." Turning to glance over my shoulder, I realized I couldn't see jack shit. Not even the subtle reflections from the other inmates and firefighters' coveralls.

Shit, we'd gone too far away from the group.

"Barker, come on. Let's just go back. You'll get your shots when we're back with the group."

My anxiety was already rising from potentially being this close to a wild fire. That shit was unpredictable and I wasn't about to get caught in something I had no idea how to get out of.

He ignored me completely and set off in the direction of the thick smoke, the reflectors on the back of his coveralls slowly disappearing from view. Panic flooded me, my mind being torn in two different directions of wanting to go back to try and find our group or follow after Barker to make sure nothing bad happened to him.

The guilt would eat at me if I went back to the group and left Barker behind to potentially run into trouble without any help. He was being an idiot, true, but no one deserved to go out like that.

Quickly darting through the trees, I caught up with him just as he was coming up to a small overhang. The heat was intense the closer we got to it, and soon, flames were dancing wildly among the dry brush.

My hand shot out to instinctively grab at the back of his coveralls. "We need to go back."

He raised the camera up to his goggle-covered eyes and snapped a few pictures. "Damn, this is *so* cool. You ever see anything like this?"

"No," I admitted. "And I don't really want to. Come on, let's go."

I tugged at him and tried to force him to come back with me, but all it really did was get him to tell me to 'fuck off' while he snapped more photos. My skin felt like it was melting inside of my suit, the heat intense enough for sweat to trickle down my back.

Barker pulled himself out of my grasp in order to move along the overhang, bypassing a tree that was half-rooted out of the soil and hanging over the empty air of where the fire was. He grabbed a hold of one of the branches down close enough for him to reach, using it as a way to swing up onto the bend in the tree's trunk.

"What the hell are you doing?"

"Shut up," he said, lifting the camera again. "You'll thank me when we get extra time out in the yard—"

Beneath him, the tree gave way from the overhang and crumbled to the ground.

CHAPTER TWENTY-SIX

Ayen

"BARKER!" I SCREAMED out just as the ground beneath me crumbled, too.

I plunged down to the ground, the six feet completely knocking the air out of my lungs when I landed onto the hard dirt. A groan escaped me while I rolled onto my side, prevented from moving any further from the pack on my back.

I'm so going to fucking kill him.

"Barker!" I called out, the haze so thick down there that it was hard to see anything. Whatever he'd said about smoke being more intense at the top of that overhang was fucking wrong, that was for sure.

I didn't hear anything from him, just the fire crackling way to close for comfort.

I hauled myself up, my shoulder nagging at me from where I'd fallen on it. Quickly checking to make sure that it was still in place, I stumbled forward while patting the ground in search of my partner.

He was lying prone on his side, with part of the tree pinning him into the dirt and no other movement visible. My heart leaped into my throat at the sight, fully convinced I'd just witnessed a man dying in front of me.

Crawling over to him, I shook him a few times, relieved to see that his mouth was open and he was pulling in a few labored breaths.

"Shit, come on." I patted my hands against his chest and face. "Wake up!"

Sweat was pouring down my face and causing my goggles to fog up from both the heat of the fire and my own body's rising temperature.

Barker let out a soft groan but otherwise didn't move.

The fire was probably about fifty feet away from us, and gaining fast. If we didn't get out of here now, we were fucking cooked.

Craning my neck up to where the overhang loomed, I noted it was a steep climb and wouldn't be easy at all to make. The dirt was rich and not packed enough to help us climb it. The second our hands dug into it, it was going to crumble away just like the tree had.

The air was too hard to see down further but maybe the incline tapered off enough for us to climb up it again.

"Okay," I said to myself, and threw my bag off of my shoulders to give me more room to work. I tucked both of my arms under Barker's armpits in order to heave him out from under the branch that was pining him. "Come on!"

My boots dug down into the dirt as I pulled, leaving deep tread marks that helped with me pushing back and counterweighing the branch.

Finally, when I was able to tug him free, he collapsed into my lap like dead weight. I panted and swiped a hand over my brow.

"Barker, you gotta get up." Slapping his cheek a few times did absolutely nothing. Not even earning me a groan.

He wasn't much bigger than me, but I had barely any muscle on me to begin with.

How the fuck was I going to carry him to safety?

Suddenly, my memory from earlier snapped into me.

I put my hand to my hip where the radio was still attached. Relief washed over me strong enough to bring tears to my eyes. I owed that man a fucking kiss, despite whatever the fuck was going on between us.

Tugging the communication device off my belt loop, I pressed the side button and said, "Help! We need help! We're near the fire!"

There was a pause of silence on the other end that felt like an eternity, but finally, a crackling response came back that I could barely make out.

Fuck, I needed better signal.

Clipping the radio back at my waist, I grabbed Barker again and pulled him up with me as I stood. Adrenaline was pounding through my veins, allowing me to drag him slowly as I followed the incline.

The popping sound of wood and embers exploding nearby had me jumping and stumbling as I tried to pick up the pace. This was not where I was going to die. Not after all the shit I'd been through in my life.

Getting taken out by the stupidity of someone else was not only ridiculous, but downright unacceptable as a way to die. If

I was going to kick the bucket, it was going to be on my own terms. Not from some dumbass trying to one up the rest of us while endangering himself and dragging me along with him.

About fifty feet from where we'd first landed, I grabbed at the radio again and screamed into it. "Help! Near the fire!"

Finally, a clearer response came. "*Who is this? What direction?*"

"Gonzalez and Barker! I think we went west!"

I fucking hoped we did. If I was sending them in the wrong goddamn direction, I was going to be so pissed at myself.

"*West?*" The voice repeated.

Stopping under another overhang, I slowly lowered Barker down to the ground and ripped the pack off of his back. I had the contents of it emptied out all over in record time and dug through them to find one of those forest ranger compasses that Mac had sent us off with.

Finding it, I held it up toward the canopy of trees, trying to pinpoint the sun through the dense smoke overhead.

"*Hello?*" The voice called again.

I put the speaker up to my mouth. "I can't find the sun." My voice cracked.

It was getting harder to breathe in the smoke billowing from the burning foliage around us. I coughed into my scarf a few times, trying to clear my lungs in order to talk again.

There was a brief pause on the other end to the radio, and then a familiar voice was talking to me.

"*Ayen, what way are you facing the fire?*"

Fuck, I wanted to cry.

I pointed the compass toward it. "North. Barker's passed out."

"*Use your whistle.*"

"Hurry," I begged.

"*Whistle, Ayen.*"

With a shaky hand, I pulled it out from where I'd tucked it under my coveralls and brought it up to my mouth. Then, with the biggest lungful of air I could manage, I blew like my life depended on it. At this point, it did.

CHAPTER TWENTY-SEVEN

Jackson

"OVER THERE!" MAC called out, but I was already running for it.

The radio was clutched so tight in my hand that I knew once I let go of it, there would be a permanent impression left behind.

The whistle was faint, followed up with Ayen's soft voice saying, *"Did you hear it?"*

I lifted the radio up to my mouth. "I'm

coming."

I crashed through overgrown brush and tangled saplings that left scratches sliced into my cheeks and hands. Behind me, I could hear Roxy and Mac and whoever else had heard the distress call following closely behind.

Giving that radio to Ayen had been an impulsive move, but one that had ultimately given me peace since I wasn't going to be able to watch over him while we split off. Now, I was regretting not simply forcing him to partner up with me and dealing with his attitude later.

Another whistle sounded off, this time much closer than the last one. I pivoted and headed for it, the smoke becoming much denser as the heat from the fire was growing more intense.

"Ayen," I called into my radio again.

He was coughing as he said, *"Are you almost here?"*

Fuck, I was never letting him out of my damn sight again. I didn't care how much of a temper tantrum he threw. He was going to be stuck to my side like a fucking glue trap until this god forsake program was over with.

"Jax!" Mac called. "I think I see them!"

Roxy's bark had me completely turning away from the direction I'd been heading in and moving deeper into the thick smoke.

She led us to a steep incline just as Ayen blew on his whistle once more from right down below us. He was coughing loudly by the time I leaned over to see him kneeling down in the dirt with the contents of his pack scattered around him and another inmate passed out next to him.

"Ayen!"

His head snapped up, his body wracking with more coughs.

I swung my pack from my shoulder and threw it down onto the ground. Ripping through it, I tossed a long tether rope to Mac and twisted around to find the grappling clips to go with it.

Roxy barked again and danced between us both as we worked, clearly anxious that she couldn't get down there and rescue Ayen herself.

"We're going to have you tie this around him, Ayen," I called down to him. "You're going to need to lift him up from there to help us pull him up over this incline."

"Okay..." His cracked voice was fucking killing me.

Focus, Jackson.

He needs you fully functional.

Mac tossed one end of the rope down to him with a large slipknot already tied into it. With the other end, he walked backward around a large tree trunk and wound it around, coming back over to me to collect two clips that he attached to his belt. I handed him a set of gloves and shoved my own hands into a pair.

"Tell us when you get that around his waist," I called down to him again.

"Do I just..." He began to choke again.

Fuck—with the way the incline was curved over them, it was creating a sort of vacuum seal for all of the smoke to collect under and not rise to dissipate into the sky like it should have already.

"Just put it around his waist for me." I held back from ending that with 'baby' by the skin of my teeth.

If I wasn't so good at catching myself before it was too late, I realized that breaking the news to Mac that I was sleeping with one of our inmates at a time like this would go down as one of the dumbest possible decisions I could ever make while staging a rescue operation.

"Okay..." he said.

"You do it?" I asked.

"Yes."

I stood and grabbed onto the rope, pulling the tension until it was taunt. Leaning back over to look down at him, I discovered Ayen was already trying to lift the other inmate up from the ground. His body was shaking, the other man's dead weight clearly tough to bear.

"That's it, just a little bit more," I encouraged.

Mac and I strained as we pulled on the support line. The angle was awkward and not at all ideal for a proper load haul operation but we were working on borrowed time and trying to find a better solution was a risk I wasn't willing to take with Ayen involved.

Mac took the brunt of the weight while I brought up the slack, keeping the tension around the trunk as tight as possible while we hand-over-handed it.

Finally, when the inmate's head popped up over the side of the incline, Mac leaned backward in order to allow me to let go of the rope.

Dropping to my knees, I fisted my hands tightly in the inmate's coveralls while hauling him up the rest of the way over. He was still passed out cold, but with a few quick taps of his cheek, his eyes fluttered under his lids.

Still alive.

Good.

With quick movements, I slipped the rope off of the inmate and loosened it up enough to toss back over the side to Ayen.

"Tie that around your waist. We're going to help you walk up the side—"

I was cut off by him dissolving into a deep coughing fit, choking on the smoke surrounding us to the point where he collapsed back onto the ground. He was bent over on his hands and knees, trying to pull in as much air as possible.

"*Fuck,*" I dug through my bag again.

"Jax, stop. We just need to get him over here." Mac grabbed my shoulder, trying to pull me back up. "Put on the rope, Ayen!"

"He can't *breathe,*" I snapped, jerking

away from him.

"If we spend time looking for a breathing apparatus then he's as good as dead. We need to get him up here *now* before he passes out."

I was inches away from tearing my fucking hair out. Both sides of my brain were screaming for two different things: jump down there and rescue him by hand or try to find him something to use to breathe into. Neither side was interested in following Mac's orders, no matter how much sense they made.

My fear was making me act irrationally, to the detriment of Ayen.

"Ayen," Mac called again. "Get the rope around you and we'll pull you up."

I crawled over to where the incline dropped off. "Ayen, just put it around your waist, sweetheart, and we'll pull you up."

His hand fisted in the dirt, slowly inching forward to where the rope was. Tears and sweat were pouring down his face to the point where he was having a hard time seeing where he was going. He patted around on the dirt, feeling for the rope.

"To your left... yes, right there," I said. "Now, put it around you... that's it."

I stood quickly, grabbing at the slack and waiting until he finally was able to get it around him. Once he tugged it twice to get it snug around his waist, Mac and I yanked on the other end hard enough that I felt my shoulders strain.

If Mac couldn't tell how desperate I was to get him up before, he certainly did now with how quickly he was having to change his hand-over-hand and toss the extra rope back away from his feet while I used both of my hands together for longer strokes to choke up on.

Ayen grabbed at the side of the incline, his hands digging down into the dead grass and dirt to help us haul him over the side. He collapsed instantly the second he was over, his legs still dangling off precariously.

I tossed the rope and dropped to my knees to grab him, scooping him up into my arms to drag him the rest of the way onto safer ground. He fell into me, becoming dead weight the moment I had my arms tightly secured around him.

I brushed my hands over his face, the grime from the smoke and dirt leaving streaks across his beautiful face. The relief at seeing him still alive and breathing was unmatched, overtaking me so hard and fast that it practically knocked the wind out of me.

When I'd first heard that distress call, my entire world felt like it'd suddenly caved inward. I hadn't wanted to believe it, having only given him my radio as an overprotective safety precaution that my stupid possessive self needed to fulfill in order to actually walk away.

I never thought he'd need to use it.

Never in a million years.

If I had, he would've never left my side today.

The fear that had completely stolen all other sense of rational thoughts from my mind was nothing like I'd ever experienced in my life. Not even when my father's alcoholic rages resulted in Carter and I walking away with black eyes and bruised bodies.

I never *ever* wanted to feel like that again. My heart was already outside of my body and being carried around by a man that I'd only know for a short time. And coming face to face with the reality of that fact was both startling and mind-boggling.

When Ayen's eyes blinked open, they were unfocused. His mouth dropped open to try and suck in as much clean air as he could.

Finally, he mumbled, "Jax..."

"You're okay." Tears leaked from my eyes as I brushed more grime from his face. "You're okay. I got you."

And I'm never ever letting you go again.

CHAPTER TWENTY-EIGHT

Ayen

A SOFT BEEPING hummed in the distance, just out of reach.

The dark, inky black of forever stared back at me—a void so cold and desolate that it made it hard to breathe or move anywhere that wasn't right in front of me. I was bound to this place, unmoving and unfeeling aside from the deep searing pain of loneliness that consumed me from within.

I couldn't remember anything before this.

Who was I?

Where did I come from?

Where had I been going before I reached this place?

The unsettling thought that maybe there *was* nothing and no one that I'd been trying to find—that I *was* no one— hovered in my peripheral, pulling me down further into the darkness. I choked on it, breathed it in and let it take hold of me.

This would be it, then. I would dissolve into oblivion.

How sad.

But then, a single memory, or maybe it was a dream, foggy in recognition at first but becoming clearer with more concentration, suddenly began to flourish in front of me. Faces that I couldn't place but felt like home, voices that I could recognize even in my sleep.

And a touch that I'd become so intimately familiar with that I craved it even now...

The touch of a hand gently running through my hair, soothingly and loving.

I missed it.

I wanted to drown in it. Let it bleed into me. Filling every crevice that the darkness had frozen over and consumed and hoped that it could pull me away from this awful place.

Distant voices were beginning to break apart the silence that cocooned me in a straightjacket. Where were they coming from?

"—maybe. We'd have to wait and see."

"How long will it take?"

"I had to do a lot of sweet talking to get into his chambers, but the judge was interested in looking over the files sometime this week."

Silence.

The air surrounding me suddenly felt charged somehow.

"Will he wake up?"

The hand moving through my hair froze.

I reached out in front of me, heartbroken at the obvious fear in the voice that had stopped it. I didn't want those warm feelings to disappear and leave me trapped here with the cold darkness again. My limbs felt numb, hard to move and sore while I fought against the binds that tethered me to this place.

I wanted out. I wanted to be set free

and go to where I was meant to be.

To who I belonged to.

Wading through the never-ending void was a hard fight, the current strong as it tried to drag me under again.

A something soft touched my cheek. A teardrop that wasn't my own.

"*Please...*"

A deep breath.

A sorrowful voice.

"Please, wake up."

Where are you? I wanted to say, but my lips felt sewn shut. *Come find me.*

But there was nothing. No one to reach out to me to lead me like I wanted them to. I would have to make this journey alone, chasing after the one thing I'd been desperate to find all of my life.

I wouldn't let it be just out of reach this time. My regrets weren't going to keep me from having what I wanted. Life was too short to live in fear of the what ifs and I was tired of sabotaging myself from what I really wanted.

Fingers brushed through my hair again, giving me a sense of hope as they traced along my temple. A soft kiss placed there.

Didn't I deserve happiness, too?

Yes, is what the void answered back, the voice sounding suspiciously familiar. *Of course you do.*

Coming back into my body was nothing like the movies. It was not a slow and gradual awakening that felt peaceful or finite. It was a hard slam of my consciousness being forced back into my body that left me gasping for breath and practically rocketing off of the bed that I was lying on.

There were things strapped to my arms and on my chest, wires that got tangled when I tried to lift up my arms and shield my eyes from the blinding light above me. Tears clouded my eyes, keeping me from seeing straight.

"Ayen, *don't*." A firm hand gripped my wrist, pinning it back by my head.

Panic flooded into my system. I was being restrained just like the void had done to me.

Claustrophobia was closing in on me—

"Baby, stop." He grabbed my other arm. "Just breathe, you're okay."

My body twisted in the bed sheets, battling against the body hovering over me and trying to grab at my other arm that I flailed around wildly. Something was covering my face, tight and uncomfortable, that sent me into a blind fight or flight. The machine next to me was blaring loudly, some kind of code going off that was making me dizzy to listen to.

I want—I want...

"Shhh." Warm lips brushed along my forehead, strong fingers lacing with mine. "I'm right here. You're okay..."

My body heaved a heavy sob with the familiar feeling of safety suddenly surrounding me.

"I know, sweetheart." More kisses along my temple. "You've got to keep everything on, though. You breathed in a lot of smoke. They need to monitor your oxygen levels."

Smoke?

Memories slammed into me.

The fire.

Barker falling down the incline.

Me radioing for help.

Jackson rescuing me—

Jax.

"That's it," he murmured. "Just relax for me. You're okay. I'm right here."

The machine next to me gradually stopped screeching, settling down to a slow and steady beeping that reminded me of my dreams. I let my body relax back into the bed, suddenly feeling how tired I really was from fighting both in and out of my head.

How did I even get here?

The last thing I remembered was Jackson throwing the rope down to me and being pulled up over the overhang. My lungs still burned a bit from the memory of choking on all of that smoke. Overwhelming darkness had hit me so suddenly that I could barely piece together what happened after that.

Jackson slowly lightened up on his hold on me, his fingers coming up to brush under my eyes where tears had collected, wiping my skin clean of them. Having him here with me made it easier to be at ease again—I didn't have to worry about being claimed by that awful darkness again.

Not when I knew Jackson would be here to pull me back out of it.

When my eyes finally focused on him again, he smiled lightly at me. The bags under his eyes were prominent, as was the shadow of his facial hair coming in. He looked tired, like he hadn't slept in days.

How long had we been here for?

My arm was heavy when I lifted it, like it weighed a hundred pounds more than I remember it being before all of this. There was one of those heart rate monitor clips attached on my pointer finger, the wire falling down somewhere off my bed to the right of my hip. An IV line stuck out from the hollow of my elbow, prickling me slightly when I tried to bend my arm up to grab at Jackson.

I wanted to touch him—needed to. I had to make sure all of this was real and not a trick of my mind.

He caught my wrist easily, gently kissing each of my knuckles before placing my hand back down onto the bed next to me.

"Jax," I mumbled, feeling miserable all over again.

He planted himself down onto the bed by my hip, the mattress slightly dipping while he was being careful to keep from sitting on any of the wires that were hooked up to the other sets of machines on my other side. Those monitors displayed all sorts of confusing looking graphs, too intense for my muddled mind to make any sense of.

"I'm right here, Ayen. I'm not going anywhere."

"Promise..." More tears were collecting along my lash line.

"Oh, honey. Of course I do." He dragged the pad of his thumb under my eyes again. "I think the drugs are making you a little weepy."

Probably.

Or the fact that I almost died trying to save an idiot.

What would've happened if Jackson never gave me that radio?

Or if he never heard my whistle?

I'm certain that I'd be a piece of fried chicken by now, never having gotten to tell him that I regretted ever pushing him away, or that I—

My heart thumped.

That I loved him.

"The doctors should be in soon to check on you," he was saying, completely oblivious to my world-shattering realization. "Once they give you the all clear, then we can sit you up and get some food in you. It's been a few days, so I'm sure you're starving."

A few days?

Jesus, now I really felt bad for dragging him into my mess. Getting involved with me like this was probably never on Jackson's agenda. We'd started out by giving in to our mutually shared spark of passion, and now he was stuck tending to me at my bedside in a damn hospital.

Why wasn't he back at the program?

Why was he torturing himself by sitting with me?

Was it because I had no one else to stay with me?

"Ayen, stop."

My gaze snapped to him, catching him shaking his head at me.

"Whatever you're thinking. Stop it. I'm here because I want to be. You have no idea how worried I was about you."

How did he...?

I couldn't be *that* transparent, right?

"Seeing you down there like that." His Adam's apple bobbed visibly. "I thought I was going to lose you."

My chest tightened when his voice cracked and a thin, wet sheen grew over his eyes.

How could he cry for me when I absolutely didn't deserve it?

Him being upset over my well-being was the last thing he needed to be dealing with. Getting hurt while in his program was probably going to cost him so much more than just me lying in this damn hospital bed. I wouldn't be able to live with myself if it resulted in the program getting shut down because of my stupidity in not dragging Barker back to the group when I should've.

"You must hate me," I mumbled.

"No, I don't."

I reached up again toward his face, desperate to wipe his tears away like he had mine. He tangled our hands together instead, twining our fingers in a tight hold that he pressed against his chest.

"I will never *ever* hate you, Ayen."

"Why?"

How could he not?

I could've cost him everything. Maybe that was why he was sitting here with me in the hospital—he had no job to go back to.

His mouth opened to answer me, but was soon cut off by the door to my room sliding open. Lifting my head up slightly, I was surprised to see a tall woman walking in with a cardboard tray with two coffees in her hand.

She stopped short at seeing us, her eyes bouncing between me and Jackson before she slowly lifted a brow. She was striking to look at, her features reminding me of those high-end fashion models that would be plastered all over NYC billboards promoting some kind of luxury perfume.

"Am I... interrupting something?"

Jackson sighed, letting go of my hand and devastating me even more when he slid off the bed to walk over toward her. "No."

She offered him one of the cups and then worked her own out of the holder that she then tossed into the small trashcan by the door. My gaze was glued to Jackson as he popped the small lip of the cup up and took a generous swig of it, clearly needing the caffeine.

He needed to go home. Now that he knew I was fine and wasn't going to die and cause him a mound of paperwork, there was no more obligation to stick around.

"Ayen, it's nice to meet you," the woman said. "I'm Nina. I'm going to be handling your case."

Oh, his lawyer friend.

In response to that, I forced myself to sit up.

"Shit—" Jackson darted back over to my side of the bed. "Ayen."

His arm quickly hooked around my midsection, holding me up when I began to sag forward. Clearly, my body was still exhausted with what it had gone through during the fire, enough that I was barely able to sit up on my own. Or maybe that was from whatever drugs they'd been giving me to keep me sedated while I recovered.

Either way, it fucking sucked.

Jackson leaned away briefly to set his coffee down on the little lip of the monitor next to me, and then wrapped both of his arms around me and very carefully readjusted me back against the mattress once more.

Nina appeared at my other side, her perfectly manicured hand reaching over to press on a button on the side of my bed that slowly raised it up into a soft incline, allowing me to sit up and still lean back into it.

"There we go," she said, before stepping back.

Jackson sighed, running a hand through my hair in an absentminded way to brush back the pieces that fell across my forehead, sending a shock of pleasure racing up my spine. Him being bold like this in front of his friend was thrilling as well as a little scary. If she reported us to the Warden, we were done for.

Surprisingly, though, she didn't seem at all fazed by it and simply walked across the room to retrieve something out of her bag that was sitting in one of the reclining chairs. A file that was probably two to three inches thick was carefully held in her hand with the pages bending from how heavy it was.

She held it up toward me. "I went through all of your documents with a few colleagues of mine. They all agree that you got pretty shafted."

My cheeks suddenly felt hot. Honestly, I never thought I'd hear a lawyer say it so bluntly. Sure, I knew it just from being in this predicament and while at the time, my court appointed lawyer had been sympathetic to a point, to hear that said from someone else other than Jackson felt... well, validating.

Of course, Jackson's opinion was important to me, but sleeping with someone tended to muddle up the brain from thinking clearly.

"Nina's planning on meeting with Judge Callahan to discuss what can be done." Jackson squeezed my hand gently. "You could have a real shot in getting out of this."

Behind him, Nina nodded. "This will all be pro bono, of course, so don't worry about any of that. But going through your case file, there's some solid evidence that your defense attorney purposefully withheld that could've swung the jury in a different direction, as well as the prosecution trying to bury witness testimony in order to win their case. That's enough to get a judge's eyes on it, at least."

This was all beginning to sound too surreal to hear.

Sure, I'd imagined this exact scenario

plenty of times late at night in my cell when I let those dark thoughts get the better of me, but my fantasy rapidly turning reality was seeming to be too good to be true.

The other shoe had to drop eventually.

Right?

It had to. That was how much my luck worked.

"There is one thing," Nina went on. "About the program."

Here it comes...

God, if the program actually got shut down because of me and Barker, I was never going to forgive myself. A decade's worth of work to be put into it, only for a couple of dumbasses to fuck up and get the whole thing completely disbanded. I had no doubts that Jackson would find another path to help people as he always had, but being the cause of collapsing something that he'd taken pride in for so long would fucking kill me.

Nina's gaze darted over to Jackson expectantly.

It dawned on me then, though, that if the program *had* been shut down because of us, then why was Jackson here in the first place?

I would've assumed he'd be too angry at me to want to wait around in a hospital room for me to wake up.

There could be an argument made that he was simply waiting for me to wake up in order to yell at me, but then again, why go through the trouble in soothing me?

If he was angry at me, he wouldn't have bothered. Jackson was a good man, a compassionate one. But he wasn't *that* nice.

He slowly turned to me and sat down on the bed again, hiking up his leg so that it was resting against my side. There was no hesitation in him when he reached out toward me and dragged his hand along my forehead and into my hair once more. Clearly, he wasn't worried about Nina tattling or about her caring in general.

Though, I was kind of curious on how that conversation even went.

"Yeah, I'm sleeping with one of the inmates in my program."

"Oh wow, really?"

"Yeah, can you take a look at his case file and get the charges dismissed?"

"Yeah, sure, no problem."

How was she not freaking out?

Jackson pulled in a slow and deep breath before he spoke. "They're sending you back, Ayen."

My brows furrowed.

Sending me back where?

"To SAC," he clarified after a moment.

Oh.

And there was the other shoe.

"We're going to get you out of there, though." He blinked hard a few times, his voice growing gruff from emotion. "I swear it. You just need to hold on over there a little longer."

I had half a mind to ask him to come visit me. I'd only ever had one visitor come and see me, and that had been Alex's mom. The entire hour had been spent in silence while she cried silently to herself, her eyes fixated on my uniform and the SAC logo stitched at the breast.

Finally, when time was called and the hour was up, she'd gotten up from her seat and left without a single word said.

For some reason, that had hit harder than if she'd come to scream at me for ruining her son's life. Just watching the pain and devastation on her face as she wept was enough of a message to get across that I'd irrevocably ruined their family more than any kind of speech ever could.

Better to keep Jackson away from any of that, though. Not to mention if any of the COs that attended the program with us caught wind of it, it'd rouse suspicion.

Because why in the world would he randomly be visiting an inmate from his program in prison?

Actually.

How the hell was he visiting me now?

Where the fuck were the guards?

A light kiss was pressed to my forehead before Jackson stood. "Hang tight, okay?"

All I could do was nod and wonder.

CHAPTER TWENTY-NINE

Ayen

FALLING BACK INTO the rhythm of being at SAC was, sadly, too easy.

I'd hoped that with spending a total of just over three weeks outside of these walls that I'd somehow lost my paranoia of looking over my shoulder every five minutes to make sure I wasn't about to get jumped.

But apparently, things like that were a

hard habit to break. Maybe I never would quite get rid of that paranoia that came over me every time I felt someone brush past me while walking by, waiting for the inevitable toss up or the press of a shiv against my kidney and the whispered threat to give them all my commissary or for an elbow to be shoved in my ribs and told to fuck off.

Life outside had felt peaceful. Life with *Jackson* had felt peaceful.

Now, all I had was my tiny cell with my cellmate again. No more sunsets to watch, or clean mountain air to breathe in, or cute golden retrievers to bury their cool noses in my side. I guess the only silver lining to all of that was that we *all* got sent back to SAC, including Barker, in order to 'reevaluate' those eligible for the program.

Luckily, no one seemed inclined to blame me or bother me much, and they were more focused on being pissed off at the Warden for punishing us all collectively for the decision. Even our COs were a bit baffled by having us *all* be sent back.

And at least I had Tyson back, too.

"Sooo, what's the letter say this week?" He swung down into my bunk where I'd squished myself against the wall.

Before he could take a peek at it, I folded the few pages up carefully and smoothed them out on my lap. "Just some updates on my court case."

Which wasn't a total lie.

Since coming back here some five weeks ago, Jackson had been regularly sending me letters with updates from Nina about her meeting with the judge and whatever else was going on in the outside world. I lived for hearing from him. I was thankful that he'd even wanted to remain in contact at all.

Receiving every letter was like getting a piece of my soul to finally come alive again. I missed him deeply and often found myself daydreaming about what we could be up to if I'd just bitten the bullet and let myself be partnered with him the day of the fire.

I'd long since forgiven him for visiting Alex and kicked myself often for not talking it out with him before everything had happened. By now, the program would've been done and over with, anyway, and I'd be back at SAC, but at least I would've gotten a few more weeks with him in person.

I missed him.

Tyson nudged my shoulder. "Hey, what's—?"

"*Gonzalez!*"

My body jolted at the sound of Barlow yelling for me.

I scrambled off of my bunk and tucked my letter under my pillow. Tyson followed me as we headed out onto the platform overlooking the common area. There was a folded up piece of paper in Barlow's hand that he waved at me once he spotted me.

"Let's go. Lawyer's here."

"Knock 'em dead." Tyson slapped my ass.

Flashing him a look, I quickly jogged down the steps to the common area and followed after Barlow as he walked to the door. Once it was buzzed open, Browne appeared on the other side with a set of handcuffs ready to go. Automatically, I held up my arms and let him cuff me, waiting patiently while he attached the short bar in between my wrists to keep me from reaching out and grabbing anything on the way down.

My stomach twisted uncomfortably. Either Nina was visiting me to tell me the bad news that there was nothing she could do for me, or this was her telling me that she's actually performed a fucking miracle and gotten us a court date.

I didn't want to get my hopes up over it, but with each letter that came in with Jackson pleading with me to hang on just for a little longer, it had me wanting to.

Hope was a dangerous thing when you were in prison. It let you paint a false reality that could quickly come crashing down once the pieces of the puzzle all finally found their homes. I'd give anything to see Jackson again, even if it meant having to stay locked up for the rest of my three years left.

Barlow and Browne escorted me down to the visitor center and into a small, private room where Nina was already sitting at the table, a thick folder in front of her. She smiled at me and stood once I was brought over to her, her eyes growing a little sad when I raised my arms up to carefully squeeze into the stationary seat attached to the table.

Once the COs had the door shut, she sat back down again. "How are you?"

"I'm okay." My palms were clammy when I wiped them against my thighs. "What about you?"

She snorted. "Busy. You've got me running around quite a bit."

Instantly, I felt bad. "I'm sor—"

"Oh stop," she chastised. "I've been dying for a good case."

See, the funny thing about Nina was that she reminded me a lot of Jackson. Both of them were the kind of workers to love running themselves into the ground and did it with a smile on their faces. Sitting around and doing nothing was like a death sentence to them and the more work piled onto their plate, the better off their mental health was.

"Well, you're welcome then," I joked.

She smiled at me. "That's the spirit."

Opening up the folder, she spread out a few pages and spun them around to face me. "I've already submitted your appeal. We've got a court date on Friday. What I need from you is to go through these and read them, and then, if you agree to what's written, I need you to sign and date them."

A court date.

She really is a fucking miracle worker.

Looking back up at her, I asked, "You actually did it."

"Hey, don't give me credit yet. We've still got to meet with the judge. I'm trying to get you time served. Callahan's not one to overturn a conviction even with substantially more evidence submitted. But as long as I can get the evidence that was previously thrown out about your past history with the victim, then we have a shot at getting you out of here."

My heart thudded. "How soon?"

"As soon as fucking Friday, kid."

Holy shit.

"Like I said, though..." she went on. "We've got to meet with the judge first and see what he says. He could order a retrial with new circumstances with the new evidence submitted or he could throw out what was used previously and have us start over with what's left. It's all up to him what will happen."

Honestly, she could be talking gibberish and it'd still sound the same to me. All I was hearing was that *yes* there was a real shot that I could be getting out of here soon.

As soon as fucking Friday, like she said.

I could see *Jackson* as soon as Friday.

Blowing out a breath, I nodded at her and set my hands down on top of the table. "Okay, tell me where to sign."

CHAPTER THIRTY

Jackson

"YOUR HONOR, GIVEN that the evidence presented here was not allowed or presented at the first trial, our appeal is for a resubmission of said evidence. We find that at the time of the trial, since the evidence of the defendant's past abuse with the victim was not taken into account, nor were the circumstances surrounding the inciting incident given proper context and presented to the jury, it directly affected my client's current conviction."

Hearing Nina speaking so eloquently to the judge, and the entire courtroom, gave me the peace of mind that she was going to try her damned hardest to get the case turned over in our favor. She'd been working tirelessly on it while I'd been running around as her errand-boy, gathering whatever evidence I could while she put together a new case file to present to Judge Callahan.

The old one had been a fucking mess and tracking down Ayen's old lawyer even more so. How the hell that man was able to still practice up until last year was beyond me.

Seeing Ayen in his SAC uniform was jarring, to say the least.

My heart had sunk when he'd been walked into the court room, his head tilted down, while two COs were on either side of him, holding onto his arms like he'd bolt at any second if given the chance. The chains between his cuffs had rattled like bells and caused a chill to run down my spine—a sound I'd probably never forget.

But once he'd lifted his head up enough to allow for one of the CO's to unlock his ankle chains in order to allow him to sit properly, his gaze had scanned over the gallery and landed directly on me. Seeing his eyes light up like that had made it all worth it—the running around, the sleepless nights worrying about him, taking a leave from the program in order to help Nina pull all of this together. Every. Single. Minute.

My hands itched to hold him again. My dreams had been filled with his warm body tucked against mine, and waking up to a cold and empty bed every morning was devastating.

I didn't believe in any form of a higher power, but today I was fucking praying as if I regularly dropped to my knees every goddamn Sunday.

"Ms. Cabone, I'm inclined to agree with you." Judge Callahan's arm swept over his desk at the stacks of paperwork from Ayen's case file. "I've been going over the evidence that was previously labeled inadmissible and while I agree that adding it back in would've changed the outcome of the jury's decision to convict Mr. Gonzalez, I'm not sure I agree with a re-trial. I feel it'd just be dragging out the inevitable."

My head was growing fuzzy from not breathing. The entirety of my body was frozen, unable to move to even begin to force myself to pull in some much-needed air.

How could I when in a single second, everything could change?

This was a moment in time that I'd never forget, no matter what the outcome was at the end of it.

My gaze was glued to the back of Ayen's head, his hair shaggy and longer since that last time I'd seen him. I longed to run my fingers through it, to tangle them in the soft lengths and watch his body relax and him begin to fall asleep from the attention.

I was grateful that other than that, he didn't look any worse off than when I'd seen him in person last. Fighting with myself constantly to not show up at SAC's doors and visit him had been the biggest struggle of my life. Letters were getting me through the weeks only so much, and if he was going back to prison again today, I might just jump over the bench and fight one of the officers myself to get thrown in there with him.

"Your Honor," Nina said. "My client's been serving for two and a half years and has been a model inmate. He recently rescued a fellow inmate during a work program incident that saved both of their lives."

Judge Callahan nodded slowly. "Mr. Gonzalez."

Ayen's shoulders visibly tensed. "Yes, Your Honor."

"Reviewing your case file, I found that a lot of the testimonies that you gave were compelling. I'm not sure what caused you to get involved with a man who was almost twice your age, but upon reviewing what you said about your relationship with him, I'm really struggling to make sense of what compelled the previous court's decision with not including that background."

Ayen's head bobbed as he nodded.

"Given that it was pretty clear that you were not in a safe spot at the time of the crime, I'm compelled to dismiss you with time served and a sentencing of probation instead, which I think is what should've happened in the first place." Judge Callahan sat back in his chair. "A minimum of five years probation and a ban on owning and operating firearms. I also want you to undergo a psychiatric eval upon release and have that submitted to the courts as well."

"Thank you, Your Honor," Nina said as the gavel was slammed down on the sound block.

Ayen's head snapped to the side to look at her, clearly just as shocked as I felt.

Holy fuck, she did it.

He's fucking free.

My legs were numb when I finally pushed myself up from the hard wooden bench. Nina reached out to steady Ayen as he climbed to his feet, one of the bailiffs coming around with a key to unlock his cuffs from him.

My baby bird was coming home.

The rest of the courtroom seemed completely unfazed while the next case number was called forward, and Nina and Ayen were quickly ushered out through the same side door Ayen had come through when he'd first been called in.

I followed after them from the public side of the court, pushing through the double doors to the main entryway into the courthouse. The marbled floors echoed softly from jogging in the leather loafers that I'd stuffed myself in to blend in with the rest of the gallery.

I didn't often find myself in a suit and tie, however I wanted to make today special. I'd *hoped* today would be special.

Fuck, I can't believe he's free.

Coming around to the backside of the private rooms, I stopped short at seeing two officers caging Ayen in while they spoke to him. One of them was giving him a small box of things while the other had the cuffs he'd previously been chained in swinging from his hands.

Nina was nowhere in sight, but that meant she was probably off signing paperwork or something to make it all official or however it worked on cases like this.

Ayen clutched the box in his arms tightly to his chest, turning at the sound of me making my way down the hallway. His eyes went wide again in the same way they had when he'd spotted me in the gallery.

Forcing myself to slow into a casual walk, I raised my hand to both officers as I approached them. "Afternoon, gentlemen."

"He here to pick you up?" one of them asked Ayen.

"That's right," I answered for him.

Smoothing my tie against my chest, I brushed my arm with Ayen's when I stopped just next to him. He vibrated against me, the shaking in his body barely detectable if I wasn't standing so close to him. Thankfully, I was within arm's length if he dropped from the sudden adrenaline crash.

"Is... is that all?" Ayen asked.

One of the officers shrugged. "Just make sure you get your paperwork before leaving."

Subtly, I put a hand on the small of his back, coaxing him to lean into my side just in case he began to waver on his feet. He wasn't worrying me just yet, but as soon as the officers turned around, I was going to sweep him up into my arms so he could fully relax.

The stress of being in court, the anxiety of waiting for a decision. It was a lot to handle even if the outcome was exactly what we'd hoped for.

The box in his hands wasn't filled with much. Just a change of clothes and some personal items, most likely from when he'd first gone into jail over two years ago. Luckily, I'd done up a whole closet for him back at my place that was filled with new clothes and shoes. Some sizes I'd guessed on, but as long as he was comfortable, it didn't matter.

"Have a good day, gentlemen." I forced a warm smile on my face.

As soon as they stepped away, so did Ayen, surprising me. He bent and set his box down carefully by my feet, his SAC uniform bunching around his midsection from how oversized it was.

When he straightened up, his eyes were filled with tears. "You came..."

Oh, my baby bird.

Cupping his face with both of my hands, I brought him back in again. "Of course I did."

"You wore a suit..."

"Had to give us some good luck."

He let out a watery laugh. "A suit is good luck?"

"My tie is. But it felt a little weird wearing one over a plain t-shirt."

Ayen buried his face in my chest, wrapping his arms around my waist to squeeze me tight enough to crack my back.

"Come here," I said, and lifted him clean off his feet.

He laughed in delight, clinging to me while I spun us around a few times. We probably looked absolutely ridiculous celebrating in the middle of a courthouse like that, but I couldn't bring myself to really care.

It wasn't every day that a damn murder charge was appealed to time served and a few years of probation.

What was that in the face of spending another three years behind bars when now, Ayen could *actually* begin his life over again?

Fucking priceless, in my opinion.

I owed Nina the most luxurious vacation known to man. Hell, I owed her a brand new Mercedes and a newly built house on top of that, too.

"Guys," came Nina's very unimpressed voice. "Seriously. We're in a courthouse. Have some fucking decorum."

Ayen breathed out another laugh when I finally set him down again and he wrapped a hand around my tie to tug me down into a chaste kiss. I wanted to fucking melt against those plush lips of his.

Unfortunately, she was right, though. As usual.

"Sorry," I said, and instead, put a hand on Ayen's back again. "We all set?"

She waved a giant stack of papers at us. "Yup. You're a free man, kid."

"I can't believe it." Ayen rubbed his hands over his face a few times. "You actually did it..."

"*We* did." Nina nodded to me. "He's been my errand bitch for the past few weeks."

Honestly, I'd do it all again in a heartbeat. Even if the outcome was different than this, he would always be worth it to me. Doing *anything* for Ayen would be worth it, no matter what I got in return.

Ayen breathed out slowly, leaning back into my side once more. "I owe you guys so much."

"Just stay out of trouble, that's all I'm asking," she said.

I pressed my lips softly against Ayen's forehead. "I think we can manage that."

CHAPTER THIRTY-ONE

Ayen

JACKSON'S HOUSE IN the city was as nice as I'd been expecting it to be.

A raised ranch on a quiet cul-de-sac that was painted a light shade of yellow to compliment the ridiculously blue California sky behind it. The rest of the neighborhood was quite the same, giving that picturesque feel to it that I'd only ever seen in magazines before while waiting in line at the grocery store.

This was the kind of neighborhood that a golden retriever and a family of four made sense in, and it felt wildly disproportionate to be bringing someone like *me* into it, given my history.

But none of that seemed to matter to Jackson at all, or faze him when I practically fainted at him offering me a room at his place.

How the hell did I deserve any of this?

This morning, I'd woken up in a damn jail cell and now, I was walking up the perfectly groomed lawn of a man who had fought to free me. All of it felt too surreal to even fathom, let alone believe that it would be my life for the next however-long Jackson decided to keep me around.

Carrying my little box of worldly possessions with me up to the red front door, I felt a rush of relief roll through me when he unlocked it and ushered me inside.

I loved this man. So much that it was actually ready to burst out of me.

"Want a tour?" he offered.

I dropped the box by the door and grabbed onto his tie again, wrapping it around my hand twice to pull him down. "Maybe later."

His mouth was hot on mine, tilting enough to deepen our kiss and draw a moan out of the both of us. He grabbed onto me, his hands on my hips, and spun me around to press me against the wall right next to the door while his hard body ground into me.

Finding out that he missed me was the best news out of all of it.

Sure, our spark *seemed* like it hadn't

died throughout our letters, but that was all subtext in order to get around the COs reading them, anyway. Seeing it—*feeling it*—in person, was a whole different story.

One of his hands smacked the back of his front door closed and then he rapidly stripped me of my uniform and tossed both scrub pieces onto the floor. Then he was sweeping me up and throwing me over his shoulder like a sack of flour.

I laughed and kicked my feet, giddy like a fucking teenager. "I missed you, too."

He slapped my bare ass. "Ayen, you have no idea how much I've missed you."

God, that was music to my fucking ears.

I got a quick sweeping look of his house on the way back to his bedroom. It was well kept and modern looking with plenty of natural light coming in from the large bay windows in the living room. A lot of it was an open concept, aside from the kitchen that was blocked off with a thick wall separating it from the rest of the house.

My gaze trailed along the walls of the hallway when we went down it. Pictures of Jackson with friends and Roxy were all displayed, along with a few of a man I didn't recognize but who looked startlingly like Jackson in an armed forces uniform.

Carter.

I smiled at the picture. He was just as handsome as Jackson was.

The hallway disappeared in place of the walls of Jackson's bedroom where I was tossed unceremoniously down onto the bed.

Another laugh bubbled up from my

throat and I clumsily grabbed at Jackson to pull him up onto the bed with me, not caring that he was halfway through trying to get himself out of the *incredibly* well-fitted suit he was wearing.

Damn, I need to find an excuse to get him back in that again.

His lips found mine again while one of his hands grabbed onto my shoulder to press me back down onto the mattress. It was soft under me and felt like a damn cloud with how thick the duvet was.

I parted my lips for him, welcoming him in and tangling our tongues together in a deep kiss. He wrapped his large hand around my cock, stroking it lovingly and like we had all the time in the world.

Which... I guess, we really did now.

There was no rush for us to come together before the inevitable clock rang, signaling time was up. We didn't need to be afraid of getting caught by the COs and dragged apart and convicted of something as stupid as giving in to our own emotions.

We had all the time in the damn world to have each other and there would be no one in our way that could stop us.

Jackson trailed his warm lips down my body until he parted my legs and dragged his tongue over my fluttering hole.

Threading my fingers through his hair, I arched my back with each thrust of his tongue inside me, wetting me all around, softening my hole, and lapping at the underside of my balls when he came up for air.

"Missed you." He nuzzled his nose against my inner thigh, inhaling deeply and squeezing the backside of my knee.

"Please," was all I could manage to say between my garbled thoughts and the pleasure that was racing through my veins.

I was being overtaken by all of the intense emotions—my want for him, the desire to keep him close to me and never ever let him go, and the love that I was drowning in that was dying to be let out.

He seemed to know exactly what I meant because before long, he was leaning back from me and shedding the rest of his clothes off and tossing them somewhere onto the floor at the foot of the bed.

He wrapped his hand around one of my ankles, holding onto it while he leaned across the bed to grab something out of the drawer and toss it onto the bed next to me. Snatching it, I lifted it and smiled at seeing the fresh and unopened bottle of lube.

"Just for me, huh?"

He grinned, running his hand up and down my leg a few times. "To be fair, I figured you'd want to nap first."

"Not after seeing you in that suit."

He laughed. "I'll keep that in mind the next time I wear it."

"Just make sure you bring this with you, too," I said, tossing the small bottle back at him.

He brought my foot up to his lips and pressed his mouth along my sole in tiny kisses, following it until he reached my ankle. Him worshiping me like that was melting me down to my bones. The devotion this man showed to the smallest things when it came to me gave me a sense of pride in myself that I'd long since thought was dead.

How in the world I'd been lucky enough to meet him, let alone entangle myself with him like this, I'll never know. But there wasn't a goddamn thing in this world that I was going to do that would mess this up again.

I was tired of pushing him away when all he'd ever done was take care of me and treat me the way I'd always been desperate for. Jackson was a good man, one that I absolutely didn't deserve in the slightest.

From here on out, though, I was going to do everything in my power to earn him.

I loved him too much to let him get away.

He gently set my leg back down and flipped open the cap on the lube, slathering a generous amount onto his fingers and circling them around my hole a few times. A deep groan bubbled up from my chest when he slid two fingers inside me, easily finding the spot that drove me fucking wild.

He stroked his digits back and forth a few times, opening me up just enough to add in a third.

I squirmed on his fingers, wanting more than just the few fingers moving inside of me. I needed *all* of him.

"Jax," I pleaded.

"Fuck, look at you," he murmured. "Just as pretty as ever."

The praise had my gut twisting pleasantly. Enough to make my toes curl.

He pulled his fingers out of me with a soft 'pop' that had me clenching around air instantly. I missed the feeling of being filled, and my patience grew thinner by the second. I'd waited so damn long to have him again that now that we were finally here and just at the precipice of finally being together again, it was driving me insane.

Thankfully, he didn't keep me waiting long and was soon dragging the head of his cock along my hole to get himself nice and lubed up while he stroked the rest of it along his base. The head of his cock slipped in easily, opening me up once more while I bore down.

He grabbed at the back of my thighs with both of his hands, holding them apart while he thrust into me a few times, getting deeper and deeper with each pull of his hips.

I was dizzy with pleasure, the feelings overwhelming my body in a way that being wasted and high at the same time was.

I loved it.

I was addicted to it.

"You always take me so good, Ayen."

He let go of my legs to lean back over me, curling his arms around me in a protective cocoon and encasing me with his body.

I dug my nails into the muscles of his shoulder blades, holding him tight against me while he sunk deep enough that his hips were flush with my ass.

He took his time with me, working himself in and out of my ass with the kind of care that a long time lover would take with their beloved. He kissed me like one, too, like fucking me wasn't enough. He had to brand me with his very essence and seep himself down deep into the core of my bones so that he could never leave.

I wanted to wear him like a tattoo imprinted into my skin that it would eventually scar over. That way, I'd never forget him or us and what we shared together.

Because we truly did have all the time in the world to be together like this. Not even an act of God could pull us apart at this point.

I came with his name on my lips, feeling the full body rush of my orgasm stealing the air out of my lungs and replacing it with his as he breathed into me.

"Fuck, baby," he whispered, his hips clapping against me until he shuddered and warmth filled me.

Jackson peppered my face with soft presses of his lips, covering every inch until I was sure that my face was covered in them.

"I love you." The words came tumbling out of me before I could stop them, my mind and emotions too caught up in all of this.

"Oh, Ayen." His forehead rested against mine. A soft smile crossed over his face. "*I* love *you*. Stay with me?"

My eyes prickled with tears. "Of course I will. As long as you'll have me."

He grinned. "Guess you're stuck with me indefinitely, then."

I'd take it.

Not a bad deal at all.

EPILOGUE

Jackson

READJUSTING THE COMFORTABLE weight of my gear once more, I looped my bag up over my shoulder and secured the straps across my chest.

A hand slapped against my shoulder twice, hard enough to make an audible sound. "Looks like it's going to be a long one, today."

I glanced out at the group of new

inmates that had come in just last week and were already moving into their next phase of training.

I nodded and nudged my fellow coworker, Mac, with my elbow. "You make it sound like you're going to be slacking off today."

"Can you blame me? Your boy's got everyone running on a tight leash these days."

Amusement trickled through me. "Scared he's going to make me scold you?"

"Wouldn't be the first time."

I slapped him with one of my gloves. "Get to work, then."

With a huff, Mac sauntered off to go join the rest of the firefighters gearing up. Roxy's barking had me craning my neck to look across the crowd of inmates, following her bouncing form in between the gap in the inmates' groups.

She was following along diligently as Ayen's keen eyes roved over the inmates, checking everyone's gear and adjusting some as he passed on through. His dark t-shirt clung to his slender frame, filled out nicely with a delicious layer of new muscles from lifting heavy things all day. His jumper pants, held up at his shoulders by thick suspenders, hugged his bottom half in such a good way, one that made me drool.

My baby bird wasn't such a baby anymore.

Pride swelled in my chest, not for the first time today. He'd been taking over our program days more often lately, and seeing him flourish like this was incredible to watch. He was a natural leader, even if he second-guessed himself sometimes. He led with a compassionate hand, a rare thing in this field nowadays but so much more needed.

Once he cleared the last of the inmate checks, he made his way over to me, Roxy merrily bounding after him, her tongue hanging from her mouth happily. He patted her head lightly, a small smile playing on his lips.

"Hey you," I greeted, bending down to grab Roxy when she got close enough and rub her sides, cooing words of praise and love over her smiling snout.

"Everyone's all set."

"Good." The gold ring on my left hand shone in the sun when it caught the light just right as I passed a hand over my dog's head. I smiled at it, the new addition feeling right at home.

Glancing over, I caught the sight of Ayen's matching one just as he pulled a glove over his hand. "We all set?"

"Yup." I stood up straight again, casting a glance over his shoulder to make sure everyone was preoccupied before I leaned in and pecked his lips. "Are you?"

He breathed out a laugh, cheeks suddenly dusted with a soft rosy tint. "Yeah. You sure you want me leading this one today?"

"I think you're more of an expert on the 'getting lost in a forest and finding your way out of it' than I am at this point."

He grinned, shoving me lightly. "He has jokes today."

"What can I say, I love your smile."

Ayen let out a soft sigh. "You need to

stop or I'm going to drag you back to our cabin."

Like that was even a threat. I'd toss the rest of the day's itinerary out the window to throw him over my shoulder and head back to our cabin for the rest of the day. Getting married a few weeks ago had done nothing to slow down our libidos.

In fact, it had made them worse in my opinion.

"Behave," Ayen mumbled, most likely sensing my fast growing dirty thoughts. Or simply seeing the way my pupils were already dilating.

"Since you asked so nicely," I said, quickly pressing my mouth to his lips again.

Honestly, at this point, we couldn't be blamed for being all over each other. We'd just come back from our honeymoon, so we could blame it on that at least.

Someone clearing their throat nearby had us breaking apart quickly. Looking over, I spotted Mac giving us both a look, his brow arched, that suggested we'd better get going.

I patted Ayen's hip lightly, nodding forward at the inmates.

"Lead the way, Boss."

He laughed. "Oh, I could get used to that."

As he sauntered off with Roxy in tow, I took up the rear, and shouldered up with Mac who was busy running through a checklist that Ayen had assigned to him earlier that morning. His hand quickly flicked over the paper with his pen, checking things off as we leisurely followed behind the group slowly moving toward the edge of the trail.

"All right!" Ayen called out. "Stick with your partners and make sure neither of you get left behind. If you get lost, use the radio or your whistles to signal to us where you are. Keep track of landmarks so we can locate you quicker!"

Pride swelled in me when the group of inmates murmured their acknowledgement and then marched forward together in a tight group. On either side of them were their COs, keeping a close eye on all of them just in case they decided to lash out or do anything ridiculous. It rarely happened but once in a while one of the inmates got uppity and it was a real threat to those determined to make good on their time here. Mostly, we'd had a stunning success in this program and we'd like to keep it that way for years to come.

"He's doing good up there," Mac said, lifting his head up from the clipboard finally.

Yes, he really, really was.

I was so proud of my little-but-not-so-little birdy.

Our future together was bright and I couldn't wait to see what came next.

Thank you for reading Jackson and Ayen's story.

Oh, and if you enjoyed this book, maybe you'll do me a huge favor and leave a review. Even a few words would mean the world to me, and it also helps other readers find the stories you love.

For more in the Smokejumpers series of sizzling firefighters, watch for Xavier, a continuation of Gage and Xavier's story, coming soon!

In the meantime, why not check out some of the other books in my backlist. A handy list is on the very next page! ☺

Love,

~Evie Riley

OTHER BOOKS BY EVIE

Federal Protection Agency

Mason
Rafe
Ryzen
Cooper
Noah
Damien
Sebastian
Gabe
Logan

Ruthless Empire

Courting Danger
Chasing Danger
Kissing Danger

Smokejumpers

Hawke
Cyrus
Jase
Gage
Jackson
Xavier

Jasper Springs
Cade
Dawson
Drew
Grayson
Riley
Mitch

From The Edge
Shattered
Runaway
Jaded
Rescue
Hidden
Tormented

Gray Vale Pack
His Fated Mate
His Wounded Warrior
His Healing Heart

ABOUT THE AUTHOR

Evie Riley is a prolific, neurodivergent author known for her captivating MM romance novels. She has gained a significant following and topped the LGBT+ action and adventure bestseller charts with her series.

Evie's writing style often explores dark and gritty themes where her men must overcome difficult obstacles in their search for love, but she has also ventured into sweeter small-town romances, incorporating tropes like enemies-to-lovers, friends-to-lovers, age-gap, and forced proximity. She is known for crafting engaging romantic suspense novels and has a knack for creating interconnected series worlds that keep readers invested.

Interestingly, Ms. Riley has hinted at exploring new genres, such as Alien Omegaverse Romance, in the future.

Outside of writing, she enjoys spending time at the beach and has a quirky personality, described by her partner as ranging from cute to deadly, depending on her blood-chocolate levels.

Evie spends her nights writing bad boys in love, and her days wrangling the sweet boys she loves.

www.ingramcontent.com/pod-product-compliance
Lightning Source LLC
Chambersburg PA
CBHW061050210726
48294CB00001B/80